Lucid

Ari Lohr

ISBN-10: 069260765X

ISBN-13: 978-0692607657

Contents

Chapter One

The Beginning

The black 2005 Honda Accord swerved around the corner as a girl with a purple jacket crossed the street.

Lucy swung her head to the right, dropping her book bag on the hard concrete below. She bent her whole body down to pick it up, and looked up, noticing the speeding object. She sprinted as fast as she could away from it.

She was too late.

The Honda slammed into her body, shattering her bones in a heartbeat. The driver sped along as he turned past another corner, the tires screeching and leaving a trail of blood. A hundred kids gathered around in a circle, their teachers trying to keep them calm. One sophomore of another school named Isaac Crowley pushed people aside as he rushed over to Lucy, hunching his body down and placing his hand on her wrist. Three teachers approached the scene and the kids spread apart, leaving-

Dead.

Isaac realized it just as soon as the teachers pushed him aside. His best friend, his life, his soul, ended in an instant as Lucy began to go cold, her soul leaving her body. He reached into her pocket and pulled out her lucky charm, and held it tightly in his hand as tears began to well in his eyes. He clenched his fists in both anger and desperation as he was pulled away from her, and he knew that this was the last time that he could see her. He caught one last glance of her, then-

Isaac woke up in a cold sweat, tears gliding down his face. He sat up and glanced at his clock. It was 7:00 A.M. He climbed out of bed, getting dressed in his favorite outfit-a red shirt and some average, boring blue jeans. He slid to the kitchen with his socks and grabbed a box of cereal, along with a bowl, filling it to a brim. He poured in some milk and nervously ate his breakfast, recapping the events of the dream.

I walked to the bus stop and saw Lucy drop her book bag. A car swerved around the corner. There was no time to scream as she got run over and the car sped away. I leaned over her.

He decided to leave it at that as he finished his cereal bowl and rinsed out the remaining bran flakes. He swung his backpack over his shoulder, walked out the front door, and headed to his bus stop, which was conveniently located beside another school. That was his favorite part of the day, mainly because he got to talk to his friends. But there's one person in particular that he wanted to talk to today: Lucy. He headed up the hill and took a left. He walked a bit further, but was stopped dead in his tracks.

The same Honda Accord as he had seen in his dream sped along at sixty miles an hour, and Isaac ran around the corner to the school. The ever-growing danger of what happened in his dream built up in real life, and he turned just in time to see Lucy drop her book bag, but she wasn't on the street. She was standing on the sidewalk, chatting with a few of her and his friends. The car zoomed past Lucy and drove straight over a puddle, drenching him with dirty rainwater. He shook a bit off and walked further, waving to Lucy and her friends.

"Yo, what's up?" He shouted, and they waved back. Lucy approached him and scanned him up and down, finally saying, "That car got you drenched. Sorry 'bout that... he he." Isaac returned her remark with another laugh and sat down on the grass beside the school.

Hurlhurst Elementary School was a large, old building made of crumbling bricks and clay. While the bricks were abundant, they were strictly for decoration. In the instance of an earthquake, all of the bricks would fall off the building, stripping it down to bare wood. Even not counting the bricks, the school didn't have a strong structure. It could've easily burned down, or even have been flooded in the instance of heavy rain. Luckily, it didn't rain much in Phoenix, Arizona. In fact, water could be hard to come across sometimes.

Isaac glanced at his other friends and invited them to sit around him, gesturing with his hand to the grass next to him and Lucy. "Come along, all and mighty, for I have a story to tell," he said as everyone sat down, now just a little bit inquisitive about what he had to say. "I had the craziest dream earlier this morning," he began as he described every detail about the dream. While he was available to joke around about it, it still was a little bit eerie to him that he had saw the same black Honda earlier.

"It sped around the corner, and I could only watch in horror as Lucy dropped her book bag. She picked it up and ran, but by the time she had gotten up, the car was already on her, crashing into her."

Isaac added a lot of emphasis on the word "crash." It was extremely difficult for him to say, but he forced the words out anyway, continuing with his story the best he could.

"I heard the sound of her bones crack viciously as the car ran into her. Sadly it sped away, but I didn't care about that. I had run straight to Lucy, pushing through a crowd of high schoolers that had formed in the blink of an eye. Whenever I got to her I instantly put two of my fingers on her wrist and waited, praying inside my head for a pulse."

As he said this last part he turned his head to face Lucy, and he could see that she was slightly affected by what was being said. He continued anyway, because he knew that deep inside Lucy wanted to hear the ending.

"Three adults pushed me aside just as I had realized that she was dead. Beforehand I had grabbed her lucky charm and was clenching it in my fist as I walked out of the crowd, getting one last glance of her, lying in a pool of blood. And then, well, I had woke up. And here I am now."

"Wow... it's hard to think about how quickly a life can end, how easily a whole world can turn upside down for one person, well, good thing it's just a dream!" Lucy replied, now clutching her lucky charm in her palm. Isaac could sense that she was a bit shaken, and she was lightly shivering. He got back up just as the bus arrived, and they all climbed aboard, sitting in their usual spots in the back.

As the bus rode along, the impact that the Isaac's story had on everybody slowly faded, and other topics began to pop up. Of course, these were less serious. They spent a whole five minutes arguing over which was better: Coke or Pepsi? In the end almost all of them agreed that Coke was better, much to Isaac's disgust.

Then there was the gossip. At Mears High, the school where Isaac went to, gossip was a normal thing. There was a constant worry about drama over someone, although if you hadn't done anything that wasn't ordinary, then there was no real worry. The kid that had constant rumors around him was Andre Gonzalez. While there was a general agreement that he was a smart student, he was weird. Very weird. He didn't like people and was often reclusive, though sometimes he just wouldn't stop talking about the most annoying things. Isaac thought that people were a little harsh on Andre, but he wasn't going to say anything to risk rumors being spread around him.

Lucy wasn't much of a gossiper. She was more of a person who liked to accept everybody into her life, but she didn't want to say that out loud. The world was a strange and cruel place, and she didn't want to become estranged from the school, or worse, her best friends. Although, she did know one person who was willing to speak truthfully; that person was Isaac Crowley. He was always accepting her, no matter what she did, and she was deeply in love with him. She kept it a secret, but she actually wanted to become his soul mate. Little did she know, he loved her as well.

Today Isaac and his friends were talking about somebody besides Andre. Melissa Blakes, (whom everybody called Melissa Belch), had just started the 30-day no makeup challenge. While everybody said that she appeared hideous without makeup, on the inside they were all thinking about how much more beautiful she had looked. They were all afraid to speak up. In other news, Andrew Wilson had broken his arm skateboarding the other day, and everyone was bound to sign his cast, since he was a senior. All in all, gossip was a common thing.

It was 7:50 and the bus had just arrived at school. Everyone climbed off of it as the first warning bell rang. Hundreds of kids stormed the halls, including Isaac and his friends. They all waved their goodbyes as they went to their lockers, and much to Isaac's delight, he shared a locker with Lucy. They had an extra minute, so they decided to chat a little bit longer.

"I wish that people weren't so mean and judging," Isaac said.

"I agree," Lucy replied, and she looked into what seemed like nothing, maybe a void.

"What's wrong?"

"Eh..."

"Come on," Isaac playfully said, "you can tell me."

"Well... Okay. It's just that, your dream that you had earlier, it really got to me. What if something like that actually happened?"

"I know, it's scary stuff, but as long as you stay safe and cautious, then you'll be fine. Don't worry bout' it. See ya later."

"Bye."

They grabbed their stuff, waved once more, and then went to their classes, preparing to start a long and monotonous Tuesday school day. Isaac thought about their conversation, and he smiled at what he had told her. He was glad that he made her less concerned about the dream.

If only he had a chance to say goodbye.

Isaac always enjoyed school, even though nobody else did. He didn't want to say it aloud, but he actually spent time studying at home. However, he still really was an average kid. At least, that's what he thought. He held his English book in one hand and his binder in the other as he walked into room 104, sitting down at his desk, next to Andre. That was the one nick that made people unsure about him at first sight: he sat next to Andre in English. However, it was small, and something that didn't affect his reputation that much.

Isaac tried his best not to tune the teacher out as she began talking. She was a new teacher, named Mrs. Peek, who had just started teaching this year. Other children took this as an opportunity to mess with her. Isaac didn't. In fact, she was secretly his favorite teacher. He took out his book and began working in his vocabulary, as that was what the teacher had instructed the class to do. It wasn't his favorite thing, but he was willing to do it over working on his book report, something that not even Andre liked to do.

Isaac shot up, startled. Andre had tapped his shoulder, so he looked over, trying to look like he wasn't talking to him.

"What?" He whispered quietly, careful not to catch the teacher's attention.

"I've done the calculations, and you need to watch your back."

"What do you mean-"

"All I can say is, trust your gut," Andre cut Isaac off, sounding casual, but intense deep inside his mind.

"Uhh... Okay, I will. Thanks for the warning," Isaac replied. Now he was just trying to get Andre to be quiet, which was successful. He decided that it was best not to listen to what Andre said, even though he had a sick feeling of danger in the pit of his stomach.

That was the biggest mistake of Isaac's life.

Isaac stretched out his arms, glancing over at his clock. It was 7:00 A.M. Luckily, he didn't have any dreams the previous night, much to his delight. The dream probably didn't mean anything. Humming quietly, he got up and did his typical morning routine, getting dressed and then eating a bowl of bran flakes. He headed to school on the same route, with a subtle skip to his step as he went along. He turned around the corner of the school and he heard the deafening roar of an engine to his right.

Isaac turned quickly. Lucy was crossing the street to board the bus, which had come early that day. She dropped her dusty, brown book bag on the paved street and picked it up. She looked to her right, and both she and Isaac saw it at the same time.

A black 2005 Honda Accord.

Its tires let out a harrowing screech as it sped along, zooming even faster than how Isaac had seen it yesterday. It was just as fast as it was in his dream. He couldn't even let out a scream as the car flattened Lucy like a pancake, her bones being crushed loudly. The car drove away, and bunches of kids emptied the building to look at what happened, much to their teachers' anger. Isaac rushed over to Lucy, pushing through the crowd and looking at her. Just like in the dream, he checked her pulse.

There was none.

Isaac felt a strange mixture of sadness and disbelief as he reached in Lucy's pocket and pulled out her charm, clenching it in his fist. The same three teachers as he had thought of earlier shoved him away and he put the charm in his pocket and pulled out his phone, calling his dad.

"H-Hi, dad... Lucy-just got ran over, and she's dead." Isaac was all chocked up with his words as he spoke. "Can, I stay ho-ho-home from school today?"

A "yes" was all that Isaac needed, and he sprinted home, tears rushing down his face. He couldn't think anymore. All he had to do was stay home, shut people out of his life. He needed some time to think. He needed some time to cry.

Chapter Two

Flames

Isaac sat on his front porch, gazing at his phone. He had been chatting with his friend for the past ten minutes.

Isaac: I can't believe what happened.

Derek: Ikr. It's crazy to know that it was the same as your dream. R u OK?

Isaac: Yeah... I was crying my eyes out earlier though.

Derek: That's fine. I was, and still am sad.

That was all that they had typed. Isaac found it hard to comprehend that his dream had come true. Out of everything crazy that had happened in his life, this took the top spot. He decided to take a while to daydream, thinking of all the other things that had happened in his life that turned it upside down. His eighth birthday party was a good example.

On his eighth birthday, Isaac invited over all of the people in his school. He expected a large turnout, knowing that young children go crazy over birthday parties. He had cake, ice cream, and plenty of streamers around, and he knew that he was going to have the best party. He had planned pin the tail on the donkey, watching movies, playing sports, and other fun games, like tag. He was determined to make it the perfect birthday party, but he was to be rudely awakened.

The party was scheduled to begin at 2:00 in the afternoon. Isaac had wanted it to start sooner, but his parents thought otherwise. He could still remember his parents' voices, telling him all about how they would never do a party that early.

"It's a Sunday, and you're asking us to wake up by 11:00? No. Assuming we woke up at 10:00, we still NEED OUR COFFEE."

Isaac slightly smiled at this thought, although it seemed impossible. His best friend had just died, and he could muster a smile? He continued to recap the day in his head. On the day of the party, April 18, he woke up, a smile plastered on his face. It seemed that nothing would spoil his good mood. He sprang out of bed, slipped his clothes on and burst out the door to his room. He ran to the living room, and sighed in awe as he looked around. Right in front of him was the same old leather couch as always, but on the glass coffee table in front of it was a pile of presents, all of them wrapped in purple paper. On his left was the walkway to the kitchen, and even from his angle he could see more presents piled on the kitchen table. In the middle of it was a large cake, shining in all of its beauty. It was three layers tall, and he could tell that his parents didn't buy it. He had never known that at least one of them could cook. On his right was the front door, but there was another glass end table beside it, with even *more* wrapped presents on it. He looked down on the hardwood floor, and he could see that there were thousands of tiny, colorful balloons, making the actual floor invisible. He craned his neck and looked at his roof, and could see green and yellow streamers hung around everywhere.

All of this contributed had massively to Isaac's good mood. There were at least fifteen presents laid out! He went into the kitchen and opened the fridge, grabbing the milk. He went and picked a bowl out of the cabinet, his favorite one, and poured himself his usual bran flakes. He sat down on the couch, pushed some of the presents aside, placed his cereal bowl on the coffee table, and picked up the remote to watch some T.V.

Six hours later, time that Isaac spent watching T.V, playing video games, and playing catch with his parents, it was 2:00. It was time for the guests to arrive. He waited, situated on the couch, bouncing his legs with giddy. The door bell sounded. Someone had arrived! He sprinted up to the door and swung it open, excited.

It was the mail man.

Isaac was disappointed, but at least there was a bright side. The mail man had brought another wrapped package, and he guessed that his parents had the package wrapped online, just like all of the others. His parents signed the paper and hoisted the package in their arms, laying it down in an empty space on the coffee table.

Another thirty minutes passed by, and Isaac began to get a little concerned. People were supposed to show up a half an hour ago, and the only people with him were his parents. He looked around, and sat back down, bored and worried.

It was 3:30. Isaac was despondent. Nobody had come to his party, and he now knew that he didn't have any friends. Almost everyone that he had given an invitation to had said they would come, so he knew that he was being stood up. He began to bawl, and got up, pulling down his streamers. His parents tried to stop him, but he was at the point of no return, and the living room would soon be trashed. He let out a scream in anger, and began to tear down more streamers. Suddenly, the doorbell rang again! He wiped his tears and walked up to it, hoping that it was a friend.

Isaac pulled the door open, and standing outside was a girl in a small purple jacket. She had seemed nervous, and he didn't recognize her. She held out her hand, and said, "hi! I'm Lucy. Sorry I'm late, I had a soccer game to play." He replied back a lot more nervously than she had did. "Oh. H-hi there... you won't find much here, but, do you like video games?"

"Of course! I love video games." Isaac could tell right away that Lucy meant it, and shook her hand, inviting her inside. They did what was planned, but mainly played video games, since they both liked that the most.

Within three hours, Isaac had made his first friend. Even thinking of the story now, tears welled up in his eyes, and he couldn't continue. There wasn't much else to say, anyway. They had a good time, became friends, and, well, Lucy got ran over years later.

Isaac was surrounded by fire. He wanted to run outside the building, but the front was blocked by even more burning wood. The alarms were beeping furiously, their deafening blasts almost distracted him, forcing him to occasionally cover his ears. He scanned his surroundings, searching for a way to evade the fire, and finally found an open corridor to his left. He turned in that direction and headed forward, along with screaming students and their teachers, trying to get them all in order. He went past them, taking a right in another hallway. He headed towards an exit door, but some debris fell from the second floor and blocked it. He began to panic now, searching for another way to go. There was nothing.

He headed for the janitor's closet. Maybe there was an air vent hidden in there. His feet rushed towards it as the fire raged on either side, and he knew that this was his last chance. The children were now all disseminated around, not listening to their teachers, so he had to push them aside as he got closer. He didn't feel very good about it, but it was either him or them, and he chose himself.

Isaac eventually made it, and he opened the door without thinking. Luckily for him, there was no fire on the other side, so he slammed it shut, locking it to keep other kids from entering. He looked up, and directly above him was an air vent, so he grabbed a stool, climbing onto it and prying the cover off.

He couldn't pry the cover off. It had four screws, so he frantically searched around looking for a screwdriver. As he searched near the door for one, he could feel the heat was stronger than whenever he entered, and he knew that the fire was drawing nearer. He had little time left, and the harrowing screams of innocent children being burned to death didn't help. After what seemed like an eternity, he finally found the screwdriver, and climbed back onto the stool, unscrewing the four screws.

One.

Two.

Three.

Fo-

The door swung open violently, and a mob of teachers and children entered. Isaac unscrewed the fourth screw and climbed into the vent, and he crawled through as fast as he could, coming upon another cover. He unscrewed it, and before he could think the hoard of children and teachers shoved him through the hole, and he fell down into grass. He sprinted forward into the street, whatever he could do to get away from the building. He turned his head to look back, and saw that virtually none of the children had gotten out of the air vent. The fire seemed to spread from child to child as all of them burned to death. Isaac could smell burning flesh, and he pulled out his phone, dialing 911. He knew that it was too late; almost all of the children had died or were going to die, and the building was totaled, but he called anyway. The fire could spread.

Isaac sat up, inhaling frigid air and immediately laying back down. It was extremely cold, and he had chills from last night's dream as well. It was 7:00 in the morning. He wrapped a blanket around himself and did his best to get dressed, wearing a jacket that he only wore two to three times a year. It wasn't often cold in the heart of Arizona. He headed downstairs, doing his usual routine; eating bran flakes, hanging out, then leaving to catch the school bus. He took the same turns as he always did, going to the bus stop as he did every school day. There was only one difference.

Lucy.

Isaac tried his best not to think about her as he walked inside the building, where he guessed all of his other friends were. It had a heater, but never air conditioning. It was something he resented about it.

The day went along normally. No one seemed directly affected by the death of Lucy, although school seemed a bit less fun than before. People seemed to be just a subtle bit more solemn to Isaac. Maybe it was just his brain playing tricks on him.

English was once again interesting. The teacher assigned the same assignments, but it was Andre that Isaac was interested in. He decided to see what would happen. As he predicted, during vocabulary work, Andre tapped his soldier, and he seemed a lot more nervous and sweaty than last time. His hands shook as he spoke.

"Lucy's death wasn't a coincidence to me. My calculations were correct. I can't say much, but I do know that you need to go inside the school tomorrow."

Isaac decided to listen to Andre this time. The next day he went inside the school, and it made sense. It was freezing again. He was sitting by himself, (his three other friends all got e-coli from a small dinner), so he had little to do but tittle his thumbs, think, do homework, and play on his phone. It was actually quite enjoyable to him.

Just as he opened a game on his phone, a buzzer sounded overhead. It was the fire alarm. Isaac was about to go through the front door, but just as he approached it a pile of debris fell from overhead. He went around for the back door, but the same thing happened. He knew exactly what this was.

Isaac ran into the janitor's closet, and immediately searched around for a screwdriver. He couldn't remember where it had been in his nightmare. The fire raged ever closer as he grabbed it, immediately placing it on the screws, unscrewing the threads. The door opened again, and teachers and students burst through. He still pressed on, and the same thing happened as earlier. He unscrewed the second cover, and was forced through it. He smelled the aroma of burning flesh again, the shrieks and screams from dying children haunting him. He dialed 911 again, and he took one last look at the burning building. Suddenly, he realized something very important.

Andre had told him to go into the building.

Chapter Three

Trust

Isaac eventually found out that school was cancelled because of a gas leak, so he headed home. A few hours later, as he was thinking about Andre's words, he decided to take a break and watch T.V. He began to flip through the channels.

"Hey there kiddos! I'm guppy the walrus, and I will kill your pare-"

"OLD SPIICCCEEEEE II'MMM ONN DDRRUUUGGSS OOHH MMAAHH GGAWWDDDDDD!"

"Everywhere you look, everywhere there's a home-"

"Today on, Animal Planet, APES!"

"Earlier today, a local Elementary school burned-"

"I can't believe you! This is Hell's Kitchen. Why did the chicken cross the road? Because you didn't fucking cook it!"

Wait.

Isaac turned back a channel to watch the news.

"Police aren't quite sure what caused the fire just yet, but arson seems to be the most plausible option."

This news was enormous to Isaac. It had all made sense. Andre had told him to go into school the next day, and his dream had come true. It was the same for the car, and Andre had been acting strange before that day as well. That couldn't all mean something, could it? Andre couldn't have predicted his dreams-that would be impossible. However, Andre was pretty smart and reclusive. What did it all mean?

Isaac decided that he needed some answers from Andre. The next day, he approached him in school, practically putting him in a choke hold. "Andre, what are you not telling me?" He had decided to use the passive-aggressive form, to seem like he wasn't hurting Andre, but he did mean business. Andre replied with his usual nervous speaking pattern. "I'm so sorry. I didn't know that the fire would happen. I just wanted to say that it would be... cold."

"Well, do you have anything else to tell me?"

"Yeah... so far your dreams have been happening, right? Well, um... I was thinking... that you could wake yourself up before it happened. That would stop it, right?"

That answer seemed plausible to Isaac. Andre told him to go inside because it would be cold, and who could predict an arson? He trusted Andre enough to know that he wouldn't commit arson.

Right?

Isaac decided to take Andre's advice. Later that day, he found himself suddenly surrounded by darkness. He wasn't sure how he had gotten there, but he did remember finishing school. He looked to his left, then his right. He wasn't sure if this was real or fake, so he kept walking, feeling a bit nervous. Earlier, Andre had said told Isaac to trust his gut. He felt like right now was a time to see if he was dreaming. He pinched the skin on his left arm.

Isaac awoke. This time he wasn't sweating very much, and he guessed that this was because the dream hadn't started completely yet. He sat up, and was glad that it was warm again. He glanced at his clock, which read 6:30, but he decided to get up anyway. To him, this was better than being bored in bed. He decided to use his extra time to watch some more T.V, (Hell's Kitchen to be exact), and laughed at how terrible everyone was at cooking. Sometimes they did well, but he still found it funny. After everything that had happened in the past few days, he badly needed to relieve his mind, in any way possible.

The bus stop had been temporarily moved to the public park while they rebuilt the school, so Isaac had to walk a little bit further than usual. He hadn't talked to his friends for a couple days, so when he got there, he was a bit surprised that they weren't already there. Then, he remembered that they had gotten e-coli. He sat down on a nearby bench, pulling out his phone and chatting with Derek a bit.

Isaac: What's up?

*Derek: Ugh... *throws up* food poisoning suckkksssss.*

Isaac: Ha. Well, I hope you get well soon.

Derek: Thx. What's happening with you?

Isaac: Andre.

Derek: Wat.

Isaac: He's been acting weird towards me lately. I mean, not typical Andre weird.

Derek: What's he been doing?

Isaac: He predicted my dreams matching up with reality. It's happened twice in a row now, including with the school. Well, actually, he wanted me to go inside the school. He made a mistake.

Derek: Dude, I'm sure that it's just a coincidence.

Isaac: Are you sure about that? I mean, twice in a row! That almost never happens.

Derek: Okay... TTYL.

Isaac: See ya.

Isaac was bothered that Derek thought it was just a coincidence, but he was also comforted by that statement. It could mean that Derek was in denial and Isaac was right, or, on the other hand, the more pleasurable option, Isaac could be wrong and it could really be just a coincidence.

Nothing notable happened in school that day. Isaac and Andre talked about normal stuff, and they almost took a liking to each other. Isaac understood why Andre hated people. People suck! They both agreed to just let things happen, and see if the dream came true the next day.

The next day, was had a chance to be the tipping point for Isaac's understanding of the dreams. If a disaster didn't happen in real life, which sadly he didn't know what to avoid, then he would get closer to understanding what these dreams were about. If a disaster did happen, then he would be back at square one.

It was 4:00. School had just finished, and Isaac was climbing aboard the bus, preparing to go back home. He pulled his phone out of his pocket, and before he knew it he was halfway to his there. All of a sudden, he heard a large noise of something breaking, and black smoke started coming out of the bus. The bus driver ordered everyone out, and Isaac had a feeling that this wasn't big enough of a disaster to be the same one as in the dream. Besides, with what he did see, they weren't similar. He texted his parents that he would walk home instead of waiting for a new bus; he had a strangely good feeling about walking home. And, Andre had told him to trust his gut!

It had seemed like an eternity, but Isaac was almost home. The sun had set earlier that night, and he was surrounded in darkness, just like in his dream. He began to walk faster. He looked back, and a dark figure was walking towards him. He walked faster. The dark figure walked faster. He went into a jog. The dark figure went into a jog. He started sprinting his legs out, and his lungs almost burst. The dark figure seemed to be faster than him, but he got to his home before the dark figure did. He quickly opened the door and went inside, locking it behind him.

The dark figure didn't come back, but Isaac was still afraid, and hardly got much sleep that night. It was 2:00 in the morning. There was a knock on the window.

It all seemed to happen in slow motion. Isaac's window was shattered into a million pieces, and the same dark figure as before climbed in. It was wearing a mask, so he couldn't see who is was. It pointed a gun at him, and he knew that he had better listen to this thing. It scooped up everything on Isaac's desk and put it all in a dark green gym bag, including the good luck charm that Lucy had originally owned. It climbed back out of the window, not laying a finger on Isaac, but he still felt dead on the inside. He had just lost his last grip to Lucy, and now all he had were memories and pictures.

The next morning Isaac informed his parents of what had happened, and they said that he had done the right thing, awarding him with ice cream. Ice cream was his favorite thing to eat, but not even that provided solace for what had happened. He was upset about his charm being lost, but most of all he was disturbed by the fact that the prediction that Andre had didn't work. Why not?

He knew that it was an impulsive and stupid decision, but he decided not to sleep that night. That morning he told Andre, who said that it wouldn't work, but he decided to try it anyway.

One day later, he got beat up at school, lost his phone, and fell down two flights of stairs.

Nothing had worked so far. Isaac was afraid of the future, and everyone around him said that it was just a coincidence. He decided that it was time to tell his parents of everything, so he approached them cautiously and then just started telling them the whole story. He decided to start from the first dream, telling about everything that had happened right to the current point. When they listened, all they did was listen and nod, with the occasional "uh-uh," or "interesting."

It had been a full fifteen minutes, but Isaac had finally told the story to his parents. They looked at him like he was crazy, and both said in unison that it was "only a coincidence." That's what everybody but Isaac and Andre thought. "Just because it hasn't ever happened before," he shot back, "that doesn't mean that it won't. Just listen to me, I know I'm right." The parents both exchanged looks, telling Isaac that they would think about it, and finally walking away. He knew that they wouldn't.

They next day Isaac woke up with his parents by his bedside. Luckily, this was the one day-in-between where he didn't dream. They told him to get dressed and he met with them downstairs.

They all climbed into their family car, a red 2003 Toyota hatchback, and drove away to a part of town that he didn't recognize. To his right were multiple different businesses, including a tea shop, a furniture store, a worn-out abandoned brick building, and what he guessed was a lingerie shop, although there was no sign. To his left was a large bookstore, an ice cream shop, a kitchen supplies store, a hair salon, and a therapist building.

They all climbed out of the car, and Isaac asked if they were going to get ice cream. His mother replied with, "close, but no. Maybe afterwards we can get some." With that line, they walked onto the sidewalk, and to Isaac's surprise, right into the therapist building.

Whenever they walked into the building, Isaac knew that he was truly alone, and the only person whom he could trust was Andre. He was despondent, and as they walked in he took a deep breath, preparing himself for what would happen ahead.

Chapter Four

Conclusions

The therapist's office had an enormous sign on both the inside and out, reading *Samantha Flugh, therapist offices.* While the building's white walls and small shape appeared inviting, Isaac knew that it wouldn't be a good experience. He tried to convince his parents that he was fine. "Why are you taking me to a therapist office?" All his mom could reply with was, "Your best friend just died, and you've been acting a bit strange lately. This'll be good for you, you'll see." With that, they entered the building, and he heaved a long sigh, knowing that he couldn't do anything about going here.

Isaac's parents walked up to the receptionist and checked in. They were right on time. They were led directly into the hallway, as no one else was in the building. He was brought into a small room with space for a leather reclining chair and another one that didn't recline. It was just like in the movies and on T.V. He lay down on the reclining chair and looked up at the white ceiling, the only place where it was comfortable to tilt his head. He was no expert on psychology, but he knew that they did this to get people more comfortable to talk, because most people don't like talking to a stranger face to face. His parents left the room, and in walked a tall brunette. She greeted him with a casual but polite "hey, Isaac." She shook his hand and sat down on the vacant chair, pulling out a large notebook and pen from her purse.

The therapist started by questioning Isaac about all that had happened. He felt no need to lie; he had already told the truth to his parents, so he started in the same scene as before: the dream. He continued to gaze up at the ceiling as he told her about the dream, the bus ride, Andre, Lucy being run over, the other dream, Andre again, and everything else that had happened until the present. All the therapist did was reply with an occasional "yeah" or "uh-uh," and she wrote down the whole story in her notebook. Isaac looked at her, and could see that she had a very grim facial expression, and knew that something was bad. She asked him to continue, so he told her about his concerns about the whole situation. She asked him how afraid he was, and he told her "a lot."

The next thing that the therapist asked Isaac was what he would do about the whole situation. This caught him by surprise. While he had earlier tried to wake himself up, that was all that he had done. That obviously didn't work. After that, he hadn't really thought about what to do next. He considered talking to Andre the next time he saw him, so he told her about that. She asked what he felt about Andre.

This question Isaac had considered many times in the past. He was unsure of whether or not Andre could be trusted, because nothing he had said had been correct, but he was all knowing it seemed. He knew about the dreams. Isaac wasn't sure what to say, so he just said that he did trust him.

The therapist took a quick glance at Isaac, and he realized that he was sweating a bit. He wiped it off his forehead discretely and continued, telling about how he was unsure of Andre. He said that he had told him to go into the burning building, and the therapist looked at him like he had three heads. "You *listened* to him?" she asked, and he replied with a "yeah..."

Life seemed to go on forever. The therapist interview continued though, and Isaac got a little bit bored. Like it was on cue, the therapist pulled a stack of papers out of her bag, and she looked at him. "We're going to play a little game, so if you were bored, well, you won't be anymore. Here's how It'll work: I will hold up an ink blot image, and I want you to tell me the first thing that you see." Isaac had heard of this game before. It would help mental health evaluation, but he wasn't crazy, so he didn't have anything to hide.

Right?

The therapist held up the first image. Isaac was unsure of what it looked like, but after a few seconds he saw what appeared to be a knife. He assumed she could tell whenever he lied, so he told her the truth.

"A knife."

"Oh."

She held up another image, and Isaac could easily tell that this one was a butterfly. Or was it a spider web?

"Sp-butterfly."

"Really?"

"Yeah, butterfly."

She raised an eyebrow and continued, showing him what appeared to be a gun. He didn't want to say that, but it obviously was. He knew that he wasn't insane.

"A gun..."

"Oh, wow."

She held up the final ink blot, and Isaac struggled immensely with this one. It looked like a combination of the devil reaching out to his soul, and kind of like a strange triangle being, trying to take him in its grasp. He once again tried to think of something else, but he had no other answers. He told her what he saw.

"Oh... OK." The therapist replied.

Isaac could kind of tell that he had failed the test, but he didn't say anything. He just looked at her as she stood up, and she began to speak. "Well, I think that we're done here. I'm going to talk to your parents about the results. Stay here, please." The therapist left, and after she was gone he slowly tiptoed to the door, pressing his ear up to it. He could barely hear what she was saying.

"Yeah... he is unsure about... test... said it was a game... knife... gun... see... mental hospital..."

What.

Isaac was dumbfounded. She wanted him to go to a mental hospital! He wanted to continue to listen, but they stopped talking and the sound of heavy footsteps headed in his direction. He sprinted back to his seat and sat down, grabbing a magazine. He didn't have time to read the title, so his parents walked in on him reading *Best Gold Chains in da' Hood.* They slightly giggled, but the full-on laugh was suppressed. He looked at them and saw that both of their eyes were red and his mom's mascara had run just a little bit. He assumed that this was another reason that they had stopped their laugh. They motioned him towards them and they all left the building without a single word. They immediately took a right and headed towards the ice cream parlor. They stepped inside the building, and the parents both asked quietly for cherry double-scoops. He asked for a simple chocolate fudge swirl.

The time at the ice cream shop was actually quite pleasant. The only problem was the looming thought in the air that Isaac might be sent away soon. He knew that he had time, so he just decided to forget about everything that had happened and just have a good time. It proved to be a great family experience, and his parents' moods improved. It seemed like everybody had forgotten about the world, and it felt good. He liked to have some time to unwind.

They licked up their ice cream and conversed in small talk, talking about the weather, the presidential election, and while the school had been shaken by Lucy's death, it was slowly but steadily returning back to normal. The murmur of school would eventually change to some other pointless gossip, and the important news of Lucy's death would be old. Isaac smiled at the remembrance of her, and he made it clear that he would make sure her name was never forgotten. While it had made him upset, and he still was, he knew that the road to recovery wasn't infinite. Every mourning cycle ended eventually, as every life did. At this thought, he erased Lucy from his mind temporarily, thinking about how his life could be ended quicker than others'. He didn't say it aloud, but he knew that he had to try something new. He needed to find a way out.

He went back to eating his ice cream and chatting with his parents, refraining from using his cell phone. This was just his time alone with them, and even though they had their moments, he still loved them dearly. He knew that they thought the same about him, and the decision to send him to a mental institution would be difficult. He would do his best to prove to them that he wasn't crazy. The weird thing was he said that he was fine, but deep in his gut he had a feeling that he was crazy. That was how it was since Lucy's death; A battle between his intuition and his brain, fighting between two extremes, with no real winners. The only way to win was to get to the bottom of the dreams.

In the middle of his thought, Isaac's parents both looked at him for a whole thirty seconds, thinking. They were acting like they were happy, but he could see the sadness in their eyes. He realized that they both must be fighting internal battles as well. Was Isaac right? Do we need to send him to a mental institution? Those were the questions that he assumed they were fighting over on the inside. He wished that he could answer them himself, but with everything that had happened lately, he wasn't sure what was right and what was wrong anymore.

Isaac pulled out his phone and took multiple pictures of the family together. He also acted like he was happy, and while they were smiling in the pictures, they all knew that no one was happy. No one said it, but tensions were actually very high. He let out a stressful sigh, trying his best to seem in a good mood. It wasn't very convincing, but his parents didn't care. They sighed too, and they tried their best to look content. It was demoralizing to him that his parents were this sad. He had never seen them so despondent where they couldn't even share their true feelings with him. At first he was angry, thinking that they were lying to him on purpose, but then he realized that they were just trying to keep him happy and safe.

Isaac's ice cream began to melt onto his hand. He was good at eating it, but his focus on more important matters had caused him to pay less attention to it. He thought of it as some kind of metaphor. The ice cream represented his life; casual, fun, and in control. Then, it slowly started melting. Everything that had seemed a normal routine felt like a blessing, and nothing was predictable. He didn't know which part of the ice cream would start melting. He didn't know where his life would lead him.

For now, Isaac just decided to leave it be and enjoy his ice cream with his parents. This might've been one of the last times he could see them.

Chapter Five

Homesick

Isaac was staring directly at Andre like he was an idiot. "What do you mean, 'you should go to a mental institution?'" He stared Andre directly in the eye, and he looked back, but he didn't seem to be looking at Isaac. He appeared to be staring off into a void, struggling to find the right words to say. Isaac asked again, and he snapped out of his trance, saying, "Sorry... it's just that you're... interesting. You're the first human that I've ever been interested in." With that, Isaac knew what he meant, no matter how messed up it was.

That night, Isaac was staring at his ceiling, trying his best to stay awake. His parents had forced him to go to bed, even though he was afraid to, but he knew that he wouldn't sleep. He would never sleep again. He knew that this was irrational, but maybe he could limit the dreams to only a few a week. It would be difficult, but it would all be worth it.

Isaac was walking to school, and a black car drove along slowly next to him. He craned his neck to the left, and saw that the windows were tinted just enough where he couldn't see inside. *This can't be good,* he thought. He quickened his pace, and so did the van. He began to sprint, and it drove faster. It turned directly to the sidewalk, and he turned around and started running in the other direction. Before he could get anywhere, the driver climbed out and grabbed him. He bit the man's arm, and the man let out a shriek in pain, releasing Isaac, who ran for his life back to his house. The man followed him, grabbing him just as he was in front of the house. The man held up a wet rag to his nose, and he tried his best to hold his breath. It didn't work. He had to breathe, and before he could scream he fell asleep.

Isaac woke up cramped and trapped. He was in the trunk of the car, and he could barely move. He felt the road beneath him, and by the speed he assumed they were by the highway. He was forced to think quickly, and he tried opening the lid.

It didn't work.

Isaac didn't know what else to do, so he wailed at the top of his lungs. He did it for what felt like an eternity, but no one came and he didn't hear any police sirens.

Finally he shot his fist through one of the lights in frustration, and it fell right out of the car and onto the street. He was right; they were on the highway. He shoved his hand through the hole, continuing to scream, but then he became quiet in the fear that the driver would hear him. A police car was eventually behind them, but its siren wasn't on, and he continued to stick his hand through. The car trailed the van and sounded its sirens momentarily, telling the man to pull over. He didn't, continuing to drive, moving a bit faster. It was a few minutes before the morning rush, so there was little traffic. The police car sounded its sirens again, but this time they didn't stop. A voice boomed, yelling "pull over" on a megaphone. The vehicle that Isaac was trapped in sped up, and more police cars showed swiftly behind. They eventually rammed the van, causing him to feel a sharp pain in his side. However, he could tell that nothing was broken. The man sped up, but the police cars blocked him, and he was forced to stop.

Isaac sat up in his bed and looked at his clock, which read 7:00. It was time to get ready for school again, but he was afraid to go. He did his usual morning routine, but he waited for five extra minutes before he left to walk to the bus stop. Whenever he did, he was extra cautious to look at the road for every second that he could

Boof!

Isaac ran directly into a jogger, and he almost fell down. He apologized, saying that he wasn't thinking, and he didn't mean to. He then continued on, determined to make it to the bus stop. He looked to his left. A black van with tinted windows drove next to him. He sprinted back home, but the man caught up to him, holding a rag over his mouth, and, of course, he woke up in the trunk. He also noticed something very peculiar: the man was wearing the same dark hooded outfit as the guy who chased him back to his house and later robbed him.

He did the same thing as his dream, punching the light out and sticking his hand through it, but whenever he looked out the hole something was different.

He wasn't on the highway. He was on a dirt road.

Isaac sweat profusely in panic. He peered to the left and the right, but it didn't mean anything. There was nothing he could do, because it was different than in his dream. It was the same van, in the same circumstances, but he was going to a different place, with no other cars on the road. He continued scanning out the hole, searching for a way out of his entrapment. He tried opening the hatch; no good. He let out a loud scream, but the only people around were him and the driver. He tried punching the lid, but it still didn't open. Nothing seemed to work, and he was dismal and afraid of the future. He put his hands to the sides and felt a lump in his pocket. As soon as he realized that it was a phone, his heart jumped. He pulled it out and turned it on. The battery was low, but it was still working. He dialed 911.

No reception.

Isaac slammed his fist on his phone, smashing the screen into a million pieces. He let out a loud shriek in frustration, knowing that he had just destroyed his only communication system. This only made him more scared, and he started to cry, longing for the loving arms of his parents. It gave him little comfort that his last experience with them was positive, eating ice cream. He never had a chance to say goodbye.

The car stopped, and Isaac could see that it was on a paved driveway. In fact, he was in a normal neighborhood, although in a town that was alien to him. Perhaps if he could escape the house that he would be trapped in, then he could find help.

Just as he thought about this, Isaac was pulled out of the car and another rag was placed over his mouth. He clawed, he scratched, all while doing his best to hold his breath, but the man was simply stronger than him, and he passed out shortly.

Isaac awoke in a small room, with only a toilet, a bathtub, and a sink. He attempted to move, but both of his arms were shackled on the sides. He felt sore, drained, and terrified as the same man as before walked in, holding a plate of what looked like lobster in one hand and a cup of hot espresso in the other. He set the cup down and began eating the lobster with a fork that was also on the plate. Isaac was particularly ravenous, meaning that it had been a few hours since breakfast. The man taunted him, saying mm each time that he put a piece in his mouth. Isaac's mouth began to water, but he tried not to show it; he didn't want to play into the man's taunts. He continued, drinking his coffee and eating more and more of the lobster. Eventually he finished the meal, and whenever he did he splashed the remaining coffee on Isaac's face. Isaac yelped at the top of his lungs as his face got splashed with the scalding hot liquid.

The man left the room, slamming the door behind him, and Isaac tugged at his chains. He knew deep inside that it wouldn't work, but he was willing to try anything to escape. He just had to be careful. He didn't know whether this man was just a bad criminal, or an expert sociopath. He couldn't take any risks, because it could be the last thing that he would ever do in his life. He felt too young to die. He continued to pull at his chains, but it did nothing to help his current situation. He looked around again, but all he saw were the same surroundings as before. The walls were covered in peeling green wallpaper, and the floor had ugly hardwood on it. He gagged.

Hours went by, and those hours turned to days. Finally, after two days, the man walked into the room again, feeding Isaac three pieces of bread and a cup of water. He unlocked Isaac's chains and stepped back, revealing a knife in his right hand. Isaac wolfed down the food, and the man looked at him, saying, "gotta keep you somewhat alive." He forced Isaac back into the chains, cutting a small slit in his palm to get him to stop squirming.

More long periods of time traveled past the world, hours, days, and to Isaac it felt like years. He wondered how long it would take for someone to find him, *if* someone would find him. He made a silent prayer to a god that he never had thought of in the pass, and a sudden realization had passed over him. He hadn't had any dreams for a week. In this thought, the man walked in and they did their normal feeding routine. Isaac wondered what the man wanted him for, because he hadn't been tortured, or worse, killed, yet.

Three more days passed by, and the man fed him again, but this time he wasn't tied back up. He clutched Isaac's arms, pulling him out of the room and into a small but cozy house, made with the same ugly green wallpaper and hardwood flooring. In all of this, the man still had black robes and a hood on. They traveled to another room, which had various instruments lying on the floor and on small tables, but these weren't for music. Isaac shuddered violently, which was met with him being slit in the hand once again.

The man lied Isaac down on a table and strapped him up with belt cords, triple-checking them to make sure they were secure. He grabbed a wet rag out of a bucket sitting on the floor, and holding it up to Isaac's mouth, covering it with the rag. Isaac tried his best not to breathe, unsure what was on the rag, but he realized that he was being waterboarded. He squirmed and let out muffled screams of various volumes as the man pressed harder. He truly believed that he was going to drown, and just as he was ready to pass out the man released the rag, dunking it back in the bucket. He then held the rag again, placing it over Isaac's mouth. He once again suffered as he was vicariously drowning, and perhaps, drowning in real life. *At least,* he thought, *it's physical pain over the mental pain in the dreams.* He was about to pass out again, but the man put the rag back into the bucket and he heaved a sigh of relief it wasn't pulled back out again. Instead, the man went on to grab a separate item; a pair of pliers. He put it on Isaac's skin and pinched as hard as he could, and he let out a holler in pain.

It went on like this for hours. The man would torture Isaac in ways that would give him pain, but wouldn't injure him, and by the time it was over he felt like dying. The man put him back in shackles, and he wept silently to himself, knowing that this would probably never end. More days went by, weeks, more torturing, forcing him to eat the worst food possible, and pouring scalding hot coffee on him. One day, as Isaac was trying to sleep, the

LUCID

ring of a doorbell awakened him. He listened as intently as he could, and this was all he heard.

"Is this...?"

"Yeah, thanks for the device. Here's the money."

"Say, have you heard about the kidnapping of a boy named Isaac?"

"No..."

"So you don't have anyone in your house... good. I was just checking."

Isaac's heart dropped. The man had just fooled someone into thinking that he was somewhere else. He continued to listen.

"Nope... There is no Isaac in my backroom."

"I never said anything about a backroom..."

"Sorry... I don't know why-"

"Sir, you're going to have to step aside for a moment please."

"Okay, listen here, hotshot. You were here to sell me torture equipment. Now get out."

"Hey! I'm an undercover police officer. Put your hands in the air or I'll shoot!"

Isaac wailed a loud scream at the top of his lungs. With the little water that he had been given, it wasn't much, but it had been loud enough to get the police officer's attention. He heard a crash and multiple gun fires. He heard some smashing as well, guessing that they were brawling. There was a lot of yelling, partially because of pain, and also because of the fight. More gunshots fired, and Isaac screamed even louder, even though the police officer knew he was in there. There were more footsteps, the sound of a door swinging open, and two people in SWAT uniforms arrived to return him to his home. There was only one problem. The man in the hood was locked up, and he wouldn't admit where the keys were. Finally, after a gunshot and a scream, he yelled, "Okay, okay, I'll tell you where the damn key is!" Seconds later another person appeared with the key and released Isaac, carrying him in their arms as he was eased into a police car. The man continued to struggle, as he witnessed, and the last image in Isaac's mind as they pulled away was the man being arrested, and before he knew it he was back at his house, knocking at the front door, standing next to four SWAT team members.

Chapter Six

Anger

One of the SWAT team members held up their hand and knocked sharply on the door. Four seconds later, Isaac's mom answered the door. She seemed exhausted, and her hair was dirty and unkempt. She was in a daze at first, but when she noticed him she began to cry, wrapping her arms around him tightly. His dad came as well, looking a bit cleaner, and he did the same thing as they brought him in. They invited the SWAT members in for some coffee, but they politely said "no, thank you." Still, everyone had to fill out some forms and answer some questions, before the SWAT team members finally left. He looked at both of his parents, finally grinning.

"It's been weeks, hasn't it?" He asked, still hugging them. Their reply caused him quite a surprise. "What... oh, what did he do to you? It's only been a day and a half!" They continued to embrace, tears streaming down their faces, and

ARI LOHR

time seemed to pass like a slug stick in a maze of salt, delicately and slowly. They took him out to ice cream again, even though it was usually just a once-a-month thing, and they had an even better time than the first one. They avoided the subject of the kidnapping, as it was over now, and they instead made small talk. They knew that he didn't want to talk about what had happened.

The feeling of being happy to be back was replaced with the feeling of tension and horror. Since not as much time had passed as Isaac thought, he was expecting a dream that night. Whenever it was the final frontier, he knew that he didn't want to go to sleep. He was aware that he would have to, but he wanted to prevent it for as long as he could.

He slowly drifted off, and he was standing by Andre. He couldn't understand what was being said, but he was overwhelmed with feelings of anger and guilt. He didn't know what Andre had said or did, but it obviously couldn't be good. He had a feeling of lost trust, and Andre began to yell back, swinging a punch. They began to fight, and he gave a fist back, right in the face. It seemed like every swing of a fist fueled his drive to punch and kick, even though he was in serious pain.

There were no winners. By the end of the fight, Isaac had a black eye and a sprained ankle, and Andre almost had a broken arm. They both gazed intently at each other, slowly backing away as they waited for the other to strike. No one threw another punch or kick, and they didn't talk to each other for the rest of the day.

Isaac woke up with a searing pain in his right eye, and wondered how the pain from his dream could transfer into real life. He pondered that thought for a moment and then glanced over at his clock, noting the time of 7:00, as usual. He climbed out of bed and got dressed, walking to the kitchen to get some cereal. He came upon both of his parents who were up, and they were making a large breakfast for all of them. He looked on the dining room table to see that various toppings were arranged about. There were strawberries, blueberries, raspberries, bananas, plates of softened butter, syrup, and powdered sugar. His parents set out another plate, one that had about twenty crepes on it, and they both chimed, "dig in!" In a singsong voice. He voiced his question about the breakfast, but he quickly dismissed it, just thanking them and getting ready to enjoy a Sunday meal with them. They made more small talk, and the crepes that he ate were delicious. He had never known that his parents could make food this delicious.

After about a half an hour, after they were done with eating the crepes, Isaac settled down on the couch and began watching T.V. He loved watching television in the mornings, especially on the weekends, and it had almost become a ritual to do this. In fact, his parents would often watch with him. Today they stayed the whole time, laughing at the jokes that only he usually laughed at. His parents seemed to pay as much attention as they could to him today, and he enjoyed it, although he knew that it would all go away eventually. There was also the harrowing thought of going to mental institution. Maybe if he convinced his parents that he wasn't crazy, then he would be able to stay.

They both looked over at him, and his dad said, "hey, I need to take you somewhere important." Isaac was a bit suspicious. Was he going to go to a mental institution now? He trusted his parents, but he was also afraid. They were extremely kind and loving to him this morning, and he figured they might be giving him a false sense of trust. "Where are we going?" He asked nonchalantly, and all his dad could reply with was, "It's a surprise." He thought about this for a moment, and decided that he could trust them. He climbed into the car, and noted that his mom wasn't going. This meant a lot to him. It meant that he could trust them, because if he was going to the mental institution, then his mom would probably be going as well, to say goodbye.

About ten minutes later, they were downtown. Isaac wondered where they were going, and he asked his dad again, who answered the same as he did before. Isaac stared out the window, perhaps longing for an answer to his hectic life, and after what seemed like an eternity they arrived at a bike shop. His eyes lit up as they stepped inside, and his dad told him that he could pick out any bike that was under 1,000 dollars. He searched around, and his eyes eventually lay on a glorious red devil. He wasn't worried about being popular anymore, but he knew that this bike would get him some points anyway. He peeked at the price tag. It was 800 dollars. He knew this was under the budget, but he thought that it might be asking a bit much of his dad. He went back to his dad and asked him about why he was getting all of this. His dad said that he wanted him to bike to school from that moment on, so he went back and grabbed the bike, bringing it upfront. He and his sole parent with him accompanied each other as they walked out after paying for it, and they both headed home in high spirits.

For the rest of the day, Isaac and his dad rode around on their bikes. His dad had had one for years, but his hadn't had one for a few months after crashing his old one, so they started out slowly, just riding around a public outdoor basketball court on the blacktop of an old middle school. Then, they picked it up by riding around the neighborhood, going up hills, and even coasting down some. Finally, it was time for the largest challenge yet. They found a wooden ramp stored in a ditch, and they brought it out onto the basketball court to test it out. His dad went first, and he aced the jump, getting three feet of air. Now it was Isaac's turn. He stared down the ramp, jumping on his bike and pedaling, moving his legs as fast as a rabbit running away from its prey. His wheels connected with the ramp and he soared in the air, going even higher than his dad, and after a million he landed on the ground below. They continued to ride on, doing even more jumps.

It was 6:00 in the evening, and Isaac and his dad arrived home to his mother cooking a cold dinner. She had almost finished, so they sat down at the table, his mother quickly serving sushi. Sushi! It was his favorite food, although they almost never had it, even though his mother could make it very well. He thought about his mom and realized that he had not done much with her, so he decided to make it a point to do activities with her after dinner. Speaking of dinner, it went very well, with the flavor of the sushi filling his mouth, making him think that everything would be okay.

After dinner, Isaac hung out with him mom a bit, reading her sections from her favorite book, *Dare to Dream*. The main character had just achieved their life goal, but found out that it was all just an illusion. They had to work even harder to get what they really wanted in life. He and his mom agreed that they wanted the main character to succeed, even though they weren't sure that she would. They were excited to read more, but the time was late, so they wound down with a little bit of comedy T.V, which was hilarious to the both of them. Eventually, it was time to go to bed, so he climbed into bed, excited for the day that would follow.

The next day, Isaac sprung up and got dressed, not bothering to look at his clock. He sprinted to the kitchen and saw that his parents had made crepes again, much to his delight. He realized that it was already 7:50 and he had woken up late, so he rushed to eat his breakfast and hug his parents goodbye, promising that he would be safe. After all, he had a bike that he could outrun people with. He rode his bike to school, doing his best to stay away from any cars that he couldn't see inside. In fact, he shied away from any cars in general. He arrived at school about ten minutes early, and saw that Andre was sitting outside, typing a story on his computer. Isaac walked over.

"Watch'a typing?"

"It's a story called 'Lucid.' I heard that you got kidnapped."

"Yeah. It was really scary, but I guess I'm still fine."

"You dream't of that... right?"

"Yeah... why?"

"Well, I wanted to tell you something important... but I didn't."

"What?"

Andre looked down, trying his best to hide the guilt in his face. "I knew that he would kidnap you, but I-"

"Wait... what?! You knew?"

"Yes! I meant to tell you, but I thought that if I did, then, well... um-the man might find out."

"What?"

"You're dream was different than real life, right?" Andre said, "So, I thought that the man was part of something... larger. He made the dream different to mess with you."

"WHAT?! SO YOU DIDN'T TELL ME?!"

"Well..."

"I SWEAR TO GOD!"

"WELL, SORRY, GOSH!"

Andre swung a punch at Isaac, and he fell backwards, firing one back. They took one look at each other and began fighting, just like in the dream. They fought back and forth, and Isaac was forced to avoid the searing pain that he had in his right eye. He guessed that there was a bruise on it. All of a sudden, Andre grabbed Isaac's arm and sunk his teeth into it, causing him to let out a holler. It was something that hadn't happened in the dream. Isaac pulled away, and they stared each other down, slowly backing away. They were both bruised and damaged, and his ankle felt twisted up and broken. Andre had fought in a different way than in the dream, and an eerie feeling descended upon him. He ran into the school, rushing to his locker and off to class. In language arts, they refused to interact with each other, and for once they didn't get called out for talking in class.

Isaac continued the day as he always did, but he was still confused. Andre knew something that he didn't, and he was going to figure it out. Was Andre trustworthy? He pondered that question as he walked out of the school building, riding home on his new bike, which had been safely been locked. He worried about his future during the ride, and he thought again about Andre. He was unsure of whether or not to continue with him, but he seemed to know all of the answers.

Time would soon prove to tell whether or not he was trustworthy.

Chapter Seven

Familiar

Isaac gazed off into an infinite void, and he wasn't sure whether or not to enter it. He wasn't sure it he could trust Andre, but he knew that he seemed to have most of the answers. He wanted to trust him, but he knew that they had gotten in a fight, and it had been a roller coaster with him. What was inside his mind? Isaac pondered this question as he rode his bike around in circles, trying to think of a way to apologize to him. Could he just walk up to him and say he was sorry? Did he have to buy him any special kinds of card, flowers, or a gift? Thinking of it just confused him even further, and he decided that the best thing to do was just apologize and say, "you were right."

The next day, Isaac woke up to his parents preparing pancakes, and he was a little bit surprised. It was different than the usual crepes, but that didn't bother him. He found it funny; large changes like dreams coming true can slowly start surprising, but small things like the breakfast food of the day being different startled him greatly. He thought about this as he sat down, his parents serving him an enormous plate of flapjacks. Luckily, he had woken up on time today, so he could finally enjoy sitting down with them and eating a nice warm breakfast, chatting and laughing. That's exactly what they did, eating their food and then watching some more comedy T.V. They were doing a slight binge of a series called *Doctor Who*, and it was the season finale. The Doctor had just revealed that he was able to regenerate, and he came back as a different doctor, much to Rose's delight. The end credits showed, and Isaac was in happy tears as he rode to school.

He arrived at the grand building, and he saw Andre standing on the steps, waiting for him. He walked up and gave a sincere apology, saying that he crossed the line by yelling. Andre apologized as well, saying that he didn't know why he had hit him. After that, he revealed that the man had held him hostage for a second, and he was forced into revealing Isaac's address. He shrugged this off, but Isaac was disturbed by this, even if he didn't show it. Andre was willing to admit his address? Did this make him not able to trust him now for sure? He wasn't certain, but he stopped thinking about it just as he heard the bell ring, so they walked inside together, parting ways whenever he got to his locker.

The day went by normally, but that night, as he lay in bed, he wasn't sure what to think. He knew that this was dream night, but he wasn't sure if he wanted to try to sleep. He was pretty sure that it didn't matter, but he dozed off anyway. He went through a quiet and tranquil night, all without a dream.

The next day, Isaac was biking to school, riding alongside Andre. They were chatting up a storm, and he realized that Andre had the coolest metal shocks, even cooler than his were. They continued to ride, passing by the abandoned library, wishing they could enter the swimming pool to their right, and noticing children playing at the public park near the school. He glanced at his mirror, noting a black 2005 Honda Accord.

A black 2005 Honda Accord.

A black 2005 Honda Accord.

He began to increase his pace. He didn't care if his legs were killing him. Andre followed close behind, and he notified him of the car. He continued to ride, constantly watching his mirror to see if the car was behind him. He turned onto the sidewalk, right by the same place where the school was, as he rushed over to the bike rack with Andre.

A bike is never faster than a car.

Isaac couldn't even think as the car slammed into his body. He tried his best to stay alert, but his ears were deafened by the sound of his bones crunching into a thousand pieces, and the last thing he saw were people rushing over to him as everything went black.

A white daze surrounded Isaac as he tried to get up, but all of the bones in his body ached as he moved, so he lied back down, looking up to see a large light. He squinted his eyes at it and then he closed them, taking a short nap.

He woke up and six people were by him: his parents, Andre, a doctor, and his friends; Derek and Max. They all had some kind of bouquet of flowers, or a box of chocolates in their hands, with Andre carrying a wrapped up gift of some kind. Isaac took turns looking at them and hearing their words, filled with sorrow, pity, and the occasional well-mannered joke. He gladly took all of the boxes of chocolates and bouquets of flowers. Lastly, he opened Andre's gift, which came with a card. Inside the box was a new case for his phone, one that he had been wanting for a while.

He gladly accepted it, and the doctor smiled warmly. He said that he would make a full recovery, and he breathed a sigh of relief, but whenever everybody walked out to let him rest he released another sigh, this one infected with tension. He knew that he would still be having dreams. But, he didn't have a dream the previous night. Or maybe he didn't remember-

7:00. Isaac could know the time without even looking now, so he shot out of his bed and got dressed, doing what was now a normal routine to him. He went downstairs and ate more pancakes with his parents, and afterwards he watched T.V with them. As he turned on the T.V, he realized the worst thing. There were no more episodes of *Doctor Who* until the new season. He had fallen into a show hole. He had no idea what to watch, so he basically sat there blankly until it was time to leave.

He arrived at school shortly after, and the day went by pretty normally. He had to deal with his annoying teachers, but he had Andre to talk to in Language Arts and his friends to hang out with at lunch, even if he had to eat the greasiest pizza in the universe. He eventually finished the day and returned back home, eating a family dinner of hamburgers and fries, and he went to bed, knowing the next day he would have to watch out for a black 2005 Honda Accord.

The next day he woke up, heading to the kitchen to see his parents cooking crepes. He walked to the dining room and had another great breakfast, giving small talk about the weather, Andre, and *Doctor Who* being over until next year. After breakfast, for the next half an hour he worked on a school project.

Just as it was time to leave, there was a knock at the door. It was Andre, and Isaac could clearly see that he had a bike with him. They rode to the school together, and everything seemed to be going great. They agreed to look out for a black 2005 Honda Accord at all times.

After what wasn't a very large amount of time, the Honda showed up behind them, and Isaac sped up, along with Andre. The car followed suit, and he arrived at the school, turning toward the bike rack. The car was less than a foot away from him, and he knew there was only one thing he could do.

He jumped aside.

Isaac bailed off his bike, leaving it for dead as he jumped away, and it was totaled in an instant. The car turned around and approached him, and again he jumped aside, shooting straight for the school building. He sprinted up the stairs, but the car had to traverse up the hill. It was just him inside now, and right behind him three large doors flied off as the car sped through. He continued to run, and he traveled up the stairs. As the car approached them, it attempted to climb up, but eventually it turned and went away.

Everyone was sent home, and Isaac was deeply shaken about the incident. For the rest of the day he sat, watching the T.V and trying to forget about what had happened. It was a normal dream day, but this time he did something different.

He had fought back.

That night, he didn't get any sleep at all. He knew that he wasn't going to dream that night, but he was still thinking about everything that had happened in the last week. It had all started with the dream about Lucy, and from there it had escalated, all the way to what was happening now. When would it all stop? *How* could it all stop? An ending seemed an impossible distance away, and Isaac felt like giving up. He knew that he had to keep fighting, although if there was no solution, then was it really worth it to fight, just to eventually die?

He didn't know what he wanted to do, but he knew that he had to let the tide go one way or the other. If he just stayed sedentary and did nothing, then he would die. He had to find a solution, and he was aware that he needed Andre's help. He gazed up at the ceiling, thinking this as he tried to go to sleep. It was no use; all of these thoughts kept him up, and in the morning he woke up tired and sore, feeling like throwing up.

Isaac's parents took his temperature, and they found out that he had a fever. He nestled down on the couch, and his parents served him crepes as he turned on the T.V. His parents accompanied him momentarily, and they all sat down together to watch their new binge-worthy show, *The Simpsons.* In this episode, Homer Simpson went to the gym and tried to work out, but he completely failed. By the end of the episode, he realized that he was just as good as he was.

It continued on like this for a few more minutes, and then his parents went to work. He was intimidated by being all alone, but he remained strong as he watched television. Later on, he emailed his teachers, asking about any homework that he had to do. Luckily, he didn't have any.

A few minutes later, Isaac vomited and tried to clean it up, eventually lying back down on the couch, turning the T.V back on. A few minutes later, there was a knock on the door, so he looked through the peep hole to see that there was nobody. He lied back down, and again there was a knock! He went back to the door, and a car crashed through the window, a millions glass shards flying in all directions. He opened the door and ran through, trying to evade the vehicle. He went towards the garage, but realized that he had no bike so instead he headed down the street, hiding in a neighbor's house. In his fear, he peeked out the window to see a vehicle facing him head on.

It was a black 2005 Honda Accord.

Chapter Eight

A Deal

Isaac was sitting with his neighbor, gazing out the window head on at a black 2005 Honda Accord. It was the same one that had terrorized him in his dreams, coming back to real life and killing Lucy, as well as trying to kill him. He sat as still as he could, and the car's engines roared violently, rushing towards him. He lunged to the side just as the car crashed through the window, shattering the glass. Its engines roared as it started up again, turning. Isaac once again went to the side, reaching into his pocket and calling 911. He did his best to avoid the car with his neighbor as he waited for the police to arrive.

A short amount of time later, two police cars showed up and sped towards the Honda, which went in the other direction. It avoided the other vehicles as it went down the road, and they followed suit, beginning a chase. Isaac couldn't see it because he was still recovering from the whole incident, but he immediately threw up in the middle of the cul-de-sack. He went back to his house, and he entered it and passed out on the couch, exhausted and not feeling well.

A few hours later his parents walked through the front door, unaware of what had happened until they saw the broken glass. They rushed toward Isaac, who was still unconscious, and they jolted him awake. They had had a great night, but the sight of broken glass made them disheveled, and they agreed to always stay home with him whenever he was sick. They asked him what happened, and their question was met with the truth, starting from whenever the car crashed through the window. They turned on the T.V and checked the news, seeing that there was a high-speed chase earlier in the day, which had resulted in the car getting away.

The car got away.

It was still out there.

Isaac shifted in his seat nervously, knowing that he would be attacked again. He wished he knew the driver, but he had no idea who it was. He didn't even have any suspects. Who could it be? He thought, staring at the broken window. He had been unsure of his safety, but now he knew that something had to be done, and fast. He was being actively attacked, and this was a war. broken window.

The next day he rode to school with his parents, as they had agreed to ride with him, and he saw that they were doing repairs on it. Class was still in session, though, so he used the detour that had been laid out. Whenever he got to his locker he hugged his mom and dad goodbye, which was met with ridicule from some students. After everything that had happened and was going to happen, petty things like slightly losing popularity didn't bother him anymore. Besides, he still had his best friends, Derek, Max, and Lucy.

Or just Derek and Max.

Isaac shrugged it off as he headed to class, hoping for a good day. In language arts, he talked with Andre about the incident, who seemed disheveled. He said that things were starting to heat up, and he was met with concern, but still no new information. He decided that the best thing to do was to analyze the dreams for any clues.

That night, he looked up at his ceiling like he always did. He was content with not having a nightmare to endure that night, but he knew the next day he would have to deal with it. He decided to just go to sleep, although he didn't. He could only think about Lucy the whole time.

The next day was pretty uneventful. He got up to the usual smell of his parents making crepes, had a wonderful breakfast, watched T.V, and was driven to school. There, he only made small talk with Andre, and he did his best to act, and feel, normal. He arrived home shortly after, watching more television with his family. Finally, after eating dinner and doing his homework, it was time to head off to bed.

Isaac knew that he would have a dream, so he did his best just to fall asleep and get it over with. All of a sudden, he was surrounded by a dense fog. He put his hand in front of his face and didn't see a thing, so he just stood still, unsure of what was to come. The fog cleared just a small amount, and he looked off into the distance to see a large pyramid-like figure, holding a very familiar person in his grasp.

Andre.

Isaac stood there and watched as the figure looked at Andre, eyeing him up and down. Finally, it began to speak. "Andre Gonzalez. I know who you are. I know where you live. Now, you're going-" Its voice quieted a large amount, and Isaac could only hear a few words.

"Listen."
"Harm."

"Me!"

The figure spoke in an extremely deep and disturbing tone, and it caused Isaac to shudder multiple times. He was about to walk closer, but the fog thickened again and he was in his bed, sitting up, looking at his clock.

7:00. Typical. Isaac climbed out of his bed and got dressed, heading to the kitchen. There, he went to the dining room and ate crepes with his parents. As usual, he didn't tell them about the dream. But, he did tell one person in particular. He was sitting in language arts and was talking with Andre whenever he told him about the dream, but all Andre did was look concerned and say that he would not listen to some stupid triangle guy.

The next day, Isaac woke up to a frigid room. He did his usual morning routine, and whenever he got to school he noticed that he was a half an hour early. The only person out front was Andre, who was typing on his laptop.

The figure came upon Andre in an instant, smashing his computer into two pieces and hoisting him up in the air. Isaac could only watch as the incident unfolded just like in the dream, and before he could say or do anything the figure disappeared, and Andre placed his head in his palms, tears gushing down his face. Isaac walked over, and he comforted him without words. He didn't know what to say, so he just stood there and sat down, patting Andre's back. He tried to say something, anything to help the current situation, but he was hushed, and for the rest of the day neither of them said a word if they could help it.

The next day, after waking up, eating his breakfast, watching T.V and heading to school, Isaac arrived and immediately went to Andre, who was sitting without any kind of laptop. He walked towards him, and he began to speak.

"Well, what happened yesterday was terrible. I don't want to say anything, except for, I'm sorry, but, what did he tell you?"

"Ahh..." Andre replied, tugging on his shirt, "He told me that I had to listen to him closely. He wanted me to go into your dream, and, well, capture you... He said that he wanted to kill you himself. He also said... to keep it confidential."

This answer satisfied Isaac, but he was still unsure. In his mind, he knew that Andre had been incorrect before, and there hadn't been any connection between the dreams yet, so why capture him in his dream rather than real life? He thought about this for a few more minutes, and then the ringing of the bell cut off his thoughts and he went inside, beginning his day.

In language arts, he was chatting with Andre, whenever a large spitball landed with a splat on his head. He turned around to see that Max had hit him with it, so he flashed a sign of confusion back, unsure why he would be hit with a spitball. It was returned with a middle finger, and he gave the same sign back, now his head filled with both confusion and anger. Just then, the teacher walked over and pulled him aside. He had to serve detention.

After more periods with Max, Isaac finally made it to the end of the day. He was about to leave whenever he realized that he had to go to detention. He approached the office and opened the door, stepping inside to see a group of three other teens. They had burly muscles and looked like they wanted trouble, and he knew that at least one of them had been arrested before. He sat on the opposite side of the room.

Time seemed to travel as slowly and carefully as a snail. Isaac put his head down on his desk, trying to go to sleep, but he couldn't. He looked up after a few minutes to see that he was being ignored, which he didn't mind, so he tried to fall asleep again. A few minutes later, as he was about to doze off, one of the burly teenagers jolted awake. He looked up to see that the teacher had walked out of the room, and he looked back at the teen, only to be punched in the face.

Three hours later, Isaac woke up, his head throbbing, and he got up from the cold linoleum floor. Nobody else was in the room. He looked at the clock and noted that it was 6:30. He was supposed to be picked up an hour ago, but he wasn't. He opened the door and walked out of the room, looking around for anyone. Nobody was anywhere, so he continued to walk around, looking for the janitor, but after a half an hour he had found nobody. He went to his locker and took out his book which he had forgotten earlier, and he continued to read it. As he settled down, he realized that he should probably call his parents, but as he pulled out his phone it was knocked out of his hand. He looked up to see a familiar figure.

It was pyramid-shaped.

Before he could think he was knocked to the ground, and the figure looked him directly in the eyes, saying, "YOU'RE UNSURE OF EVERYTHING, AREN'T YOU? WHAT'S TRUE, WHAT'S NOT, THAT'S THE QUESTION. NONE OF IT IS TRUE, ISAAC. EVERYTHING YOU THINK YOU KNOW IT WRONG. ANDRE CAN'T BE-"

The figure was pulled aside and another one appeared in its place, opening a portal and sending the other one through it. The new figure looked just like the last one, and it spoke slowly and clearly.

"Ahh... my stupid twin brother is always trying to confuse people. He tried to use Andre as a pawn, and now he's trying to use you." The figure held out its hand, and Isaac shook it. He could see the intensity in its eyes, and a fiery Armageddon, and he did his best not to look at it as he continued to listen to the strange figure.

"Well, kid, I'm willin' to make a deal with ya'. So, just shut you're ears and listen. I'm willin' to help you in your dreams, but you're gonna have to give me access to them first. Just, shake my hand again and I'll be in."

"Who are you, and why are you helping me?" Isaac replied.

"I'm Matt, and my brother's name is Holt. He's trying to use you and Andre as pawns for his ultimate plan to eventually destroy the world. He wants everyone to be his slave, and he wants you and Andre to eventually, well, die. I want to help not because I care a hundred percent about you, but because I want to help save the world. So, are ya' willin' to trust me?"

"Well, I don't know..."

"Come on-you can trust me."

"I'm sorry, but I have to think about it." In truth, Isaac had almost no trust for this figure, but he was still unsure, he slowly backed away, and the figure said, "Okay, think about it then. Until you decide, just remember, don't trust the other figure." With that, Isaac ran off, unsure of what to do and who to trust.

Time would prove to answer all of his questions.

Chapter Nine

Lockdown

Isaac walked home, still unsure of everything. Whenever he stepped inside, he saw his parents acting as if nothing had happened. They saw him and apologized a million times, saying that they had forgotten about him being in detention. They joked that it was his punishment, but there was a universal agreement that since he had never been in detention before, he would get a one-time warning. He was perfectly fine with that, and he agreed that he would never get there again. After those words they enjoyed a wonderful meal of pan fried fish, watching T.V afterwards. That night, he went to bed refreshed and content, but as the lights were turned off he was alone with his thoughts, terrified of what was to come. He knew that he didn't have a dream that night, but after everything that had happened, he wasn't taking any chances. He thought about the first figure's words that he had heard earlier. The figure had said, he thought, that Andre couldn't be trusted. Could he? Were they just being played as pawns?

These thoughts were a constant burden to Isaac. Every day he had to wake up, not knowing what was to come, and it gave him a constant fear of death. He and Andre were the only people that knew about this, and they were alone, forced to suffer in silence, only each other to talk to. He wanted answers, and he thought about the deal that he had to decide on. Should he let Matt in his dreams? It seemed awfully fishy, but he knew that he needed a change of pace, something to ease the current situation. Having someone help him would certainly make things easier, and things couldn't get any worse, so why not do it? Why not take a risk, if it could save his life, and possibly the lives of countless others around him, maybe even the whole world, to quote Matt. He pondered these thoughts as he drifted off, coming into his final resting place for the night.

The next day was a Thursday. Isaac woke up, glanced at his clock, and headed to the dining room, ready to eat yet another breakfast. He sat at the table and eagerly watched as bowls of various fruits were laid out, and finally the crepes were put down. He thanked his parents joyfully and dug in, indulging in his favorite part of the day. Afterwards, they watched television and drove off to school, beginning yet another day.

Isaac decided not to tell Andre about what had happened. He knew he was important in all of this, so he wanted to see what he would say and do. They didn't actually talk about anything new, because there wasn't really anything to say. They just made their usual small talk, and whenever the bell rang they went into the school, splitting off to their lockers. They met up again in language arts, doing their best to ignore Max as he continued to torment them. Isaac eventually gave him a mean look, but it didn't change the situation. The day still continued on, and nothing else noteworthy happened to him.

That night, as he gazed at his ceiling like he always did, he thought about everything again. He came with the conclusion of just seeing where the dream took him, and he was nowhere but everywhere, in a daze, unsure of what was up and down and left and right. He tried to look around but he saw nothing and everything again, and he realized that he had been knocked out. He waited a few more minutes and eventually got to his senses, realizing that he was inside the school building again. Everything was silent as he walked around, trying to look into a classroom. The inside window of the door was covered with poster paper, so he tried another, and then another. They were all covered. He tried going into one of the classrooms, but they were all locked. He couldn't even enter the bathroom.

After a few minutes, he paused to hear the sound of gunfire, and the sudden realization that this was a lock down dawned upon him, and he did his best to hide in a corner, utterly silent. There was the sound of glass breaking, a door being swung open, and more gunfire.

It went on like this for about five more minutes, and then there was a return fire. It had come from a police officer, hidden away near Isaac. He looked out to see the gunman wearing dark robes and a hood. It rushed off in the other direction, and the police followed suit, with him secretly coming along behind. He saw the man sprint through the front door, avoiding the shots of the police officers, and climbing into a vehicle.

A black 2005 Honda Accord.

Isaac sat in disbelief as it sped off, leaving everyone else in its dust. An "all clear" was sounded, and relieved teenagers walked into the halls, but it was announced that to accommodate for the dead, school was cancelled for the rest of the day. The teens all let out a sigh of both tension and relief, and soon after no one was left in the school, including Isaac.

7:00. That was the time every morning. That was the time when Isaac sat up, in a cold sweat and a daze, directly after a dream. He woke up and looked around, happy to see that he was in his own room again. He got dressed and did his usual morning routine, and eventually he was in school, ready to head off to lunch.

There, he sat down with Andre, who he hadn't been seen earlier due to a dentist appointment. He was happy to report a clean bill of health, but the mood quickly darkened with the news of the latest dream, casting a dreary spell on both of their days. They agreed to head for the nearest classroom, staying safe.

That night, Isaac thought about the day that was to come with terror; he wasn't prepared for a lock down. He thought about all the harrowing events that were happening, and he wished that it hadn't of happened to him. He was kind. He was smart. He was athletic. What made him so bad that he deserved this punishment? Was this all some kind of cruel joke by fate, made just to torment him, to cause him to suffer, or was there a reason? These thoughts burdened his mind as he fell asleep, not mentally prepared for what was to come.

"Lock down."

"Lock down."

The alarms buzzed as hundreds of teenagers swarmed the halls, searching for a classroom to seek refuge in. Isaac was in a panic, doing his best not to get hurt by any of them. He sprinted to a classroom, tugging at the door handle and turning it. Locked. He tried to find another door, but he couldn't think straight. People everywhere were rushing around, and he didn't have time to keep himself safe. An elbow connected with his head, and the last thing he could remember was a searing pain in his right temple, before everything quickly fell black.

Immediately Isaac stood up, looking around. It was the same setting as his dream, the same time. Soon enough he heard gunshots, and he searched for the same hiding place. He quietly waited for the police to arrive as he heard more gunshots, coming closer and closer.

The man was upon him in a flash. Isaac was shot in the hand, and he released a cry of pain at the bullet going into his body. He fought back, tackling the man as he reloaded his weapon. Before long they were clawing and screaming, with wild gunshots flying in the air. He smacked the gun with his good hand and it was sent flying, clattering on the ground twenty feet away. They both raced towards it, doing whatever they could to pass the other. Isaac was physically stronger, and he reached it first, picking it up and immediately firing it. It hit the gunman's leg, and at that moment the police came out of hiding, arresting the hooded man. Before that happened, though, Isaac reached for his hood, pulling it off to finally reveal who it was.

Max.

Max tried to kill Isaac.

Max was the gunman.

Max was evil.

Isaac was taken aback by who it was and sat down, forcing himself to calm himself. If Max, one of his best friends, could turn bad, then who could he trust? By now he almost trusted Andre, and he had always trusted Derek. Maybe he had to reevaluate his relations with people. Maybe he really had no one to talk to.

For the rest of the day he sat at home, watching T.V. Was there a secret to all of this? Was there a detail that he was missing, some kind of corner that he had accidentally cut, or did he really just have to go with the flow? What could he do to end the suffering? How could he fix everything?

The following day was a Saturday. The rain hammered outside as Isaac played video games on his new phone. He had to do something, anything, to give him a glimpse of reality. He needed to unwind, relax a bit, so he sat and twiddled around on what his parents promised would be his last phone if he broke it again. That thought gave him worry, but on the grander scale of things it was no big deal at all. It was just another way for him to hide from the truth, so why even have it?

Isaac stepped outside and walked to the street. The rain glided down his face and body as he stood, feeling the unique sensation with both his body and mind. He wondered how much longer he would get to be normal to people, and how long it would be before he would become a blubbering mess. How long did he have to last?

It felt stupid to him, but he went inside and took a test to see how long he would live. He answered all of the questions truthfully, and the number that he got was until he was 86 years old. That was how long he would live if none of this had happened. Now, with all of this, he had no idea how long he had left. He wasn't sure if he could deal with the pressure of death.

His parents called him for dinner and he came out, enjoying a fresh plate of tacos, one of his favorite foods. He did his best to act normal as he always did, eating, talking, and laughing with his parents. They chatted about normal things, like school and television, but the main topic was the shooting. It was decided that the school would be reopened on Monday, which actually made him feel relieved. He would rather be in a large crowd in his situation.

After dinner, the whole family sat down to watch some T.V. It was one of the many things they enjoyed to do together. As always, they had a wonderful time, laughing at the comedy shows, and slightly crying at the sad ones. They even stayed up late and watched a movie, although it wasn't very good.

That night, Isaac tossed and turned, unable to go to sleep. After everything that was crazy in his life, this topped the list. He was almost unsure before, but now he was certain that these prophetic dreams, or rather nightmares, were both the worst and craziest things that had ever happened to him. When would it all stop? Would it all stop? He pondered these questions as he lay down again, ready to go to yet another dreamless sleep in the pattern that he was experiencing.

C h a p t e r   T e n

Return

Max was back, facing Isaac, holding a knife in his hand. Isaac took a slow step back, turned, and ran for his life. He was taunted with chants, and they only added to his fear. "I've escaped from prison. You're gonna die!" Those words were repeated over and over, and they seemed to destroy his mind, forcing him to run even faster, even though his lungs were giving out. He climbed over a fence and pulled out his phone, turning it on and dialing 911 yet again. He was still being chased, and he struggled to keep running. He knew that he was only doing so because of a massive adrenaline rush. He wasn't about to let Max kill him. He was too young to die. He had to survive.

7:00. Monday. The dream was cut short this time, and Isaac sat up, peering over at his clock. He quickly got dressed and headed to the dining room for breakfast. In a hurry he ate his crepes and turned on the T.V, although he didn't know why he was rushing. Maybe he was just worried for what might happen the next day. After he had arrived at school he immediately told Andre of his dream, who said to always stay with someone in the same room as him. Sadly, he was told "no" by his parents.

"We're going out on a date tonight, so you're gonna be home alone tonight. There's some frozen pizza that you can heat up. Love you!"

"Are you sure guys? I feel awfully afraid..."

"Oh, you'll be fine, don't worry!"

With that, his parents were on their way, and Isaac sat on the couch and turned on the T.V. He did his best to stay alert, and he continued to look out the window. 911 was now on speed dial after everything that had happened, so he could call them at the touch of a finger. He sat perfectly still, but he was in a position where he could easily launch up and run. He decided that he would escape by going through whichever door was available.

More time went by, and he reached into the freezer, pulling the frozen pizza. He unpacked it and placed its contents in the preheated oven. Fifteen minutes later, it was ready, so he took it out and set it on the counter to cool, still ready for an attack at any minute. He reached into one of his drawers and grabbed a knife, holding it in his good hand. The other one had been shot by the gunman.

Ten minutes later, the pizza had finally cooled off, so he sliced it up and put a few of them on a plate. He looked at what he was about to eat and decided that he was hungrier than that, so he grabbed a few more slices, going back to the couch to turn on the television set. He sat and ate his meal, laughing at the comedy show that he was watching. He eased up a bit, but it would soon prove to be a mistake.

There was a violent crash, and Isaac turned his head towards where the noise had come from: the dining room. He opened the front door and stood by it, ready to run out of it, but he heard footsteps behind him, so he turned around. Max was now by the front door! Isaac had no choice but to turn around and run towards the back door, so that's exactly what he did. He quickly found out that he was trapped, so he had no choice but to climb over the fence, and into a neighbor's yard. He was followed by Max, who was directly behind him, giving the same chants as in the dream. "I've escaped from prison. You're gonna die!"

Isaac reached in his pocket for his phone, but it wasn't there. He turned to see Max holding it, saying, "Nice going, sport. Your phone fell out of your pocket. Oh well. I guess it's mine now." He continued to sprint, going through more yards. He eventually took a left turn and ended up on the street, wailing for help at the top of his lungs. No one seemed to hear him as he shouted, but he didn't stop, relentlessly trying to get someone, *anyone's,* attention. Still, no one could hear him, and his throat became dry, and it was hard for him to even utter a single sound. The fact that his lungs were virtually empty didn't help either. Yet he still kept running, adrenaline fueling him to keep on going, because he wouldn't let Max kill him. He couldn't.

After a few minutes of running, Isaac realized that he still had the knife in his hand. He turned around to face Max, and he held up the knife, not surprised to see one held up at him. They slowly circled around each other, gazing fiercely into each other's eyes, waiting for the other one to strike. Finally, Max charged, letting out a war cry as their daggers clashed, and they began to fight, hacking and slashing in a fevered frenzy. They fought relentlessly as they both began to bleed, and he could feel a thousand ounces of pain. Still, he fought back, aiming for the open areas.

Max had left his stomach open at one point. Isaac noticed this, and he put his whole body into a lunge, trying to get him in an area that he couldn't just shrug off. The knife went straight through the skin, and he could feel it going through the stomach. Blood surged out as he pulled the knife back, thrusting again in a different spot. He did this as many times as he could, because he had to make sure Max was dead. He had to make sure the battle was over. He reached into Max's pocket and pulled out his phone, dialing 911. He told the police about the whole situation, and they listened to him. The last thing that Isaac saw of Max was him being put into a body bag, thrown into the silent and solemn ambulance.

Whenever his parents got home, Isaac told them the whole story. He explained that he was ready to go out the front door, whenever he was almost stabbed in the back. He told the whole chase in detail, perfectly remembering the chants that had reached his ears. His parents didn't say a word, they just listened, and they finally hugged him and said they wouldn't let him out of their sight again. He breathed a sigh of relief at this.

That night, he couldn't get to sleep. All of the recent events had been getting more intense, and now he was in an active knife fight, in which he even got scars. He knew it was bad to think about, but he thought that it wouldn't be his last one on one fight, and maybe even not his last one with weapons.

The next day, Andre had seen the whole incident on the news, and some other people had, too. This information spread around the school like wildfire, and whenever Isaac got to the worn building he was treated as both a hero and an outsider. He was unsure what to make of it. Andre approached him and asked him to explain it in detail, so he did, starting with the dream. Other people had asked him about it too, but he made no mention of that dream, or any dreams, for that matter. He couldn't have them know that he was different. He was already estranged by everybody as it was.

Even Isaac's teachers asked him about it. Whenever they did, he gave the same doctored version as he told most other people, and they treated him like he was a recipient of a medal of honor. He even got a certificate from the principal for being such a hero. It was a great award, but inside his mind it was bittersweet. Was he really a hero, or was he just defending himself? He thought that he didn't deserve it, but he didn't say that. Instead, in his surprise acceptance speech, he said that while he was thankful for the award, he would also like to say that he was just defending himself, and he was sure that anyone could do it if they tried as hard as they could. Of course, this thought was dismissed by the staff, saying that he was a hero. Even the janitor whom he had never talked to called him a person to be honored.

Talking with Andre was the best part of Isaac's day. They talked about how the dream was different, and they agreed to keep alert at all times, no matter what was thought, no matter what they were told. They had to be ready for anything, even if it meant they had to prepare for the end of the world. Perhaps the world would end soon, and no one knew it yet.

That evening, Isaac and his parents went out to dinner with Andre and his parents. They went to a Mexican restaurant, where he ordered the tacos and Andre ordered the quesadillas. There, they obviously didn't talk about the dreams, but instead they made small talk in the beginning, and then their parents got to know each other. Isaac and Andre also got to know each other a bit more, and developed even more of a friendship. He realized he was Andre's only real friend, so he decided to be nice, because he wanted to be a kind person. He liked Andre, and he trusted him. All in all, both families had an extremely positive experience, and they agreed to meet again sometime in the future.

Finally, at the end of the day, Isaac lay on his bed, fixated on the ceiling, and he heaved a long and hard sigh. He wasn't sure what was put into it, but he knew that he had to do something. He decided that the next dream he had he would analyze, figuring out every single detail. He would avoid the bad outcome, no matter what. Eventually, he knew, he would die, so he decided that the time for action was now, in order to circumvent a premature death. There had to be a way. There was always a way.

Right?

There was always a way. That statement was said by famous astronomers, physicists, mathematicians, and other influential people. *If they found a solution,* Isaac thought, *then I can.* There had to be a way. There is a solution to everything. Everything can be explained in some way, so if he found that explanation, then maybe he could figure out what to do. Maybe then he could stop everything that had happened. Maybe then he could stop the dreams, once and for all. Maybe then he could be normal again.

Isaac released another sigh and settled underneath the blankets, doing his best to fall asleep. He was certain that he wouldn't dream, but he was still afraid to keep time moving forward. If he stopped time, then he wouldn't have another dream. He wouldn't feel the sensation of being alive, but he wouldn't dream again. He knew that it was absurd, but he wished that he knew the secret to stopping time. He wished that he could be like God.

The next day, he woke up, glanced at the clock, (it was 7:00), and he headed to the dining room. He looked forward to eating crepes with his parents, and afterwards watching T.V. That's exactly what they did. At least his mornings were predictable. At least it was one thing that made him normal. At least he could have some kind of connection to reality.

He climbed into their car, and they drove off to school. After a while, he was in front of the building, standing with Andre, and they walked in, both slowly, ready to begin yet another day of school. Another part of the routine called life.

Chapter Eleven

Rewind

It was a normal day at school. Life passed by regularly, and everything was fine. Yes, there were the dreams to worry about, but without that, everything was the same. No one was dying. There was no black 2005 Honda Accord in sight, and no pyramid-like figures terrorized Isaac or Andre.

Then time stopped.

The whole world just stopped spinning, and everyone on it came to a halt. Nothing was moving, not even time, and no one could notice it. No one except Isaac and Andre.

It had all started whenever Isaac had a dream. It appeared that the dream was a break from the worst, with him being beat up at school. That was pretty bad, but it could've been much worse. Someone could've died. Someone could've ended the whole fight, one punch in the wrong place, and someone would die, falling on the ground, wilting

ARI LOHR

away like a head of cabbage, slowly disappearing from the world, ending all reality.

Then, he woke up in a cold sweat, seeing the clock at 7:00. Everything was normal. He was mentally prepared to get beat up. It wasn't a big deal. He sprinted to the dining room and ate crepes with his parents, one of his favorite things to do, and afterwards he watched television, finally climbing into the family car after the program. They drove off to school, leaving their house behind them, and possibly his last glance of reality.

They arrived at the school, and he climbed out of the car, thanking his parents for the breakfast and the ride. He went off to see Andre, who looked distressed and flustered. "Isaac!" He said in a hurry. "I don't have much time. I'm being controlled. I can't say much, but all I know is don't trust the t-" He disappeared into a cloud of dust, and Isaac coughed violently. He was early, and no one was around to see it. He was the only one to see Andre disappear, but where did he-

Isaac was standing in an infinite void. He was surrounded by an intense pitch black, alone. He looked around, and he couldn't see anything, so he began to walk, occasionally calling out. Sadness fell over him, and he felt completely isolated. He stood where he was, not moving a single muscle; he had no idea where he was or where to go. Andre appeared next to him, and they were both relieved to see each other. They exchanged an awkward hug, and then backed off, looking around.

As they stood in huffish thought, Matt appeared, and Andre disappeared again. It gazed directly at Isaac, an intense fire in its eyes. "Sorry, but I need it to be private. Do you accept my deal or not? I need an answer now."

"Well..." Isaac replied back, unsure. "No. I don't accept your offer."

"No? NO? Do you know who you're dealing with here?" The figure began to speak in a low and menacing tone, and its color became a bright red hue. "I AM THE SPIRIT OF DARKNESS. THE STRONG WILL BE MADE WEAK, AND THE WEAK WILL FOLLOW UNDERNEATH MY DOMAIN. I WILL CAUSE YOUR DEATH, YOUR INFINITE SUFFERING. I AM THE LIVING HELL THAT YOU PEOPLE THINK OF."

The world spun around at an uncontrollable pace, and Isaac lost his balance, falling to the ground. A large pillar rose out of the ground, and they were both standing on it. It was a giant arena. The figure, which called itself Matt, shot a fireball towards him, who barely dodged it. He longed for Andre, who appeared randomly by his side. Another fireball was shot, and they both wished for some kind of advantage against Matt.

They got what they asked for. It wasn't long before they figured out that they could get anything that came into their minds. With this added detail, the fight was equal, with Andre and Isaac having the advantage in numbers. Isaac knew that if he defeated Matt, then the dreams might stop. Everything could go back to normal.

They continued to fight, and Matt was deeply wounded. The rage shone in its eyes like a raging fire, and with every second the battle got more intense. Finally, he shot up. "ALRIGHT! THAT'S IT!" The world became normal around them, but everyone was stuck in place. It was completely silent. "YOU WANT TO LIVE, THEN LIVE IN A WORLD OF NOTHING!" Matt disappeared, and everything was left the same as it was, except for one small detail.

Time had stopped.

So that was where they were now. Time was stopped, and Isaac and Andre didn't know what to do next. They walked around, touching people, trying to manipulate objects. It was impossible.

Time was stopped, so they were just as heavy as dark matter, if not heavier.

Matt came back in a fury, and he grappled Isaac, lifting him in the air. "Of course," he said, unusually happy. "You can live here, Andre, and I'll take Isaac back to the empty void, where he'll spend all of eternity. Yes. This is perfect..."

That's exactly what he did. He took Isaac back to the void and left, and he was all alone, pacing around in circles. *What do I do?* He thought. *Think... Think, damnit!* He continued to walk around, sometimes creating small entertainment for himself. Nothing could distract him of his real goal, though. How could he imagine the whole world? He didn't know every single element of the world, so he couldn't imagine it back. He tried to imagine a portal to the other world, but he could only imagine small bits and pieces of it. However, he did try to imagine Andre, and it worked. If they worked together, he figured, then they could get out of this dilemma.

They sat in a circle, trying to think of how to get the world back to normal. Finally, in blind ideas, Isaac imagined a small clock. He looked at it and noticed that it was broken, so he turned the handle to try to fix it. All of a sudden, the whole world went backwards, and they were standing in front of the school again. It was 9:00, so the bell rang. It was a normal day again. They looked at the clock and smiled, but Isaac's grin quickly changed into a frown. He needed to destroy the clock, so that it couldn't get into the wrong hands.

He kept it in his pocket until lunch. Then, he went into the boiler room. He glanced at the clock again, thinking of all the possibilities for it, but at the same time, all of the things that could happen if it got into the wrong hands. He threw the clock into the fire, and it burned up, destroying the ultimate key to time, the way to solve all of the paradoxes and problems of the universe.

Later that day, Isaac ate dinner with his parents, and he was overwhelmed with a feeling of happiness. He knew that he wouldn't have many more experiences of normality with people, so anything that could put him with people was cherished by him. He knew that he had to make the most of everything that he could use to connect with people, so he did.

Afterwards, he watched reality T.V with his parents. It was both funny and sad to see the celebrities' stupid problems, but to him it seemed frivolous. Small problems weren't as important to him anymore; these large problems were the most important things. With what he had seen, only the craziest things were important and interesting to him. There was so much to learn out there, so many things to see. He had a hunger for knowledge, but to him, being safe was more important.

That night, he lied down and knew that the next day he would get off easy, only being beat up at school. Still, he was extremely cautious, and he knew something would probably change between now and then. He tried his best to go to sleep, and actually slept well for the first time in a while.

Isaac woke up the next morning and glanced at the clock; 7:00, the usual time. He let out a small groan and got up, not excited to the school day that he had to endure. He got dressed and headed to the dining room, sitting down and patiently waiting for the usual crepes. Soon enough, all of the toppings were set down, and finally, the stars of the dish were put on the table. The family made small chatter and talked about T.V as they ate, and they actually ended up eating slower than usual, so they left as soon as they finished their meal.

The drive to school didn't take as long. Isaac and Andre had agreed to meet at school fifteen minutes early to hang out, so they did. Of course, not all of it was just for fun. In fact, most of the time they talked about the previous day's events, including time stopping. Whenever Isaac wondered how the people didn't realize that time stopped, Andre answered the question by saying that since time had stopped, they couldn't sense that they weren't moving. Technically, that meant that time could constantly be stopping. Maybe it is.

School went by pretty normally. Isaac got through all of his classes with some commendation from his teachers and peers, but that was all old news now. Instead, the whole murmur of the crowd was Amelia's new boyfriend, Stevie. Isaac and Andre chuckled about someone talking about them.

"Oh, my, gawd! So, my friend's roommate's cousin's boyfriend told me that Amelia is going out with Stevie. Hashtag Cray Cray!"

"OMG, I know, right? It's so crazy!"

During lunch, Isaac sat with his friend Derek. He hadn't talked with him for a long time, and he still wanted to be his buddy. They gave small talk in the beginning, but eventually Derek asked about the dreams that he had texted him about a while ago. Isaac said that it was just a one time thing, and he was acting paranoid. They continued to chat, and after a half an hour the bell rang. It was time to go to the next class.

At the end of the school day, Isaac's parents picked him up and they drove home. They ate another wonderful dinner, and afterwards they winded down by watching television. They stayed up late, since it would be a weekend soon.

Finally, at 12:00 midnight, the hilarious comedy movie ended, and everyone went to bed for the night. Isaac lay down and gazed at his ceiling, thinking about the sky. He wished that he could fly and be free as a bird, almost never touching down on the land below. He wished that he could explore the world, figure out space-time. But most of all, he wished that he could find a solution to the dreams. There was one out there, but it was hidden, and he would have to work hard to find it. It would be like solving a puzzle; he would have to intricately put each and every piece together, and finally, after many long hours of hard work and effort, it would be done.

That was another thing. How long would it take for it to stop? Isaac knew that if he worked hard then he could stop the dreams, but could he be killed before then? The dreams were getting worse, and he knew Matt wasn't on his side. Earlier, he had almost signed a deal with the devil!

If he wanted to get to the bottom of everything, then he had to change and intensify his strategy. He had to be innovative.

All of these thoughts burdened Isaac as he lied in his bed, occasionally tossing and turning. He wondered if there really was a solution to everything, and his mind began to wander far and wide, over hills and through tunnels, around rocks and over them, and he wondered where it would all end, where humanity and space-time would cease to exist. Could it all die out eventually? These thoughts confused and bothered him, but he still tried to think about them more. Unfortunately, before he could continue to think, all of his exhaustion of watching movies caught up with him, and he was fast asleep.

Chapter Twelve

A Sight

Saturday.

To Isaac, everything seemed trivial and dumb. He didn't say anything, but deep inside he knew that nothing mattered as much anymore. He had seen a glimpse of what lied beyond his own domain, and he had a thirst for knowledge that was unmatched, even by some of the most influential scientists of all time. He knew that it didn't make much sense, but he wanted to feel danger. He wanted to live his life. He wanted to explore, to see beyond the naked eye, to dive into the deepest oceans, or above in the heavens. He needed to experience exploration.

These thoughts bombarded his mind over and over again as he went through his day, doing all of the things that made him normal. He woke up at 7:00, ate breakfast, watched T.V with his family, and now he was doing some yard work. While most people don't like to do it, he didn't like to do it at all, especially now with his new found knowledge. Later on in the day, he decided to call Andre and vent out to him, telling him about his thoughts.

Andre listened without a single word, but only with the occasional grunt to show that he was still listening. Isaac described every single desire that he had in detail, talking about how much there really was to see. For the first time, he was actually looking forward to the dreams. He wanted to discover something new, see the world, and experience danger. And he wanted to do it with Andre. He wished that they could go everywhere, capturing all knowledge they could. He continued to explain, and Andre finally cut him off. "Isaac. Before you keep talking. I think of this everyday. I want to experience the world in the same way."

There was a moment of an awkward, but meaningful silence, and finally, Isaac spoke again. "I hope to see you in my dreams tonight," which was met with another awkward silence. "Yeah, Isaac, I see what you meant, but that was a bit funny," Andre replied, and with that, the conversation was over.

That night, Isaac stared at his ceiling and did his best to go to sleep. He was looking forward to his dreams, and he was even more excited to meet with Andre again. Eventually, he dozed off, and he finally entered his lucid world once again.

Isaac was in his normal school, in language arts class, and he was sitting next to Andre. He tapped him on the shoulder, and they saw each other and smiled. They began to chat quietly, but they did their best to look discreet. They chatted about small things, like the weather and Donald Trump, and then Isaac felt a spit ball land on the back of his neck. He slowly turned around, and he saw Max sitting in the seat behind him.

Max.

Isaac immediately raised his eyebrows in concern and raised his hand. His teacher looked him dead in the eye, and she asked him what he had to say. He told her about Max, and whenever he did she dismissed this claim, saying that he was seeing things. Even after that dismissal, he still saw Max sitting there, grinning from ear to ear, and he began to say his usual taunts. "I've escaped from prison, and I'm gonna kill you." He repeated it over and over again, and Isaac raised his hand again, saying, "How can you not see him?! He's right there."

The teacher slowly walked over to him, and she told him to come with her. They walked through the hallways and to a small room, where he was left alone. A few minutes later the counselor walked in, holding a clipboard.

"Hey, Isaac," she chimed, shaking his hand. "So, I'd like you to tell me about Max, and what you saw." "Well," he replied, "I saw him in class, and he sent a spitball to my neck. He also taunted me, saying the same things that he did whenever I was running from him: 'I've escaped from prison, and I'm gonna kill you.'" This caused her to look concerned, and she wrote something down on her clipboard. She looked back at him, walking him back to class without words.

That day, Isaac was picked up by his parents and taken out for ice cream. They looked sad, and he suddenly knew why. Immediately after, he was taken to an insane asylum. He reluctantly let himself be admitted, and he realized that he had made the stupid mistake of telling the truth to this lady.

Isaac woke up and looked over at his clock. As usual, it was 7:00, so he got up and put his clothes on, heading down to the dining room to eat some crepes. They had a great time together, and they also enjoyed watching T.V. They all climbed into the car in high spirits, and had a great drive talking and laughing. Eventually, he was at school, so he entered the building. Andre was nowhere, and he guessed that he was sick. He shrugged this thought off and walked through the school, excited for the day that was to happen.

The school day was quite normal. Isaac talked with some of his friends, including Derek, and he took two different tests. He actually got one of them back that day. He grinned from ear to ear whenever he read the grade, an "A." He had been making exceptionally good grades lately. In language arts, he also started a new unit in his vocabulary books, which proved to be quite easy. He was glad that everything in school had become just a little bit easier. Things were finally beginning to look up.

That night, after getting home from school, doing homework, eating dinner, and finally watching T.V with his parents, Isaac lay in his bed and gazed up at his ceiling, ready for the next day. He prepared mentally for Max to come back, and he made sure that he knew it was all in his head. He went to sleep content, and he hoped that the next day would be just that enjoyable.

7:00. Always that time. Every day, that was what he woke up to. He sat up and looked at his clock again, confirming what the time was. He got dressed and headed downstairs, already plotting how he was going to circumvent going to the asylum, just like he had done the night before. He went to the dining room and ate crepes with his family, doing extra well to make it last. He loved his family, and he didn't want to let go of them. He watched some television after the meal, then finally, he headed off to school in the family car.

At school, he told Andre about what had happened whenever he was gone, and then talked about the rest of the dream that was missed. He said that he could have sworn he had seen Max, and he wondered what the dream meant. He decided to ignore seeing him, and he knew that he wouldn't say anything if he really did. The bell rang, and everyone rushed off to their lockers, ready to begin the new school day.

Eventually it was time for language arts to start, so Isaac headed off to class, a skip in his step. He was excited for having his knowledge, even if Andre was the only person that he could share it with. He stepped inside the classroom, but there was no sign of Max. However, he knew that he would show up soon. He waved to Andre, who had just walked in as well, and they sat down together, opening up their vocabulary books.

The bell rang again, and their teacher began speaking about what they would do in class that day. In the beginning, they would work on their vocabulary books, and then later on they would go do some reading and journaling about them. They went off and began with their work, and everything was going normally. Isaac and Andre were also chatting quietly.

After a while, sure enough, Isaac felt a spit ball on his neck. He turned around, and there Max was, telling his usual chants. He felt a cold shudder go down his spine, but he knew that it was no big deal. Max was only an illusion, unlike most other dreams.

Isaac got an idea. He reached out his hand and attempted to touch Max's shirt, expecting his hand to go through. However, it didn't. The shirt was solid, and so was the rest of Max's body. He was there physically, but no one else could see him. He tapped Andre and turned him around. He didn't see Max, so he assumed that it was only an illusion. He decided to ignore it.

For the rest of the day, Max appeared everywhere, from the back desk in all of the classes, to in the restaurant that Isaac went out to dinner with, and even next to him in his bead. He looked up as he lied in his bed, doing his best not to think of the person that was right next to him. However, the presence was still there, and the never-ending taunts kept him up all night long. By morning, he was exhausted, but he still got up at 7:00, went to the dining room, ate crepes with his family, and went to school, with Max next to him at all times. In school constant spit balls slid down his neck, but he did his best to ignore them, disposing of them discretely and often. They bothered him, but he knew that he had to remain strong, to have endurance. He couldn't go to an insane asylum. He knew that he wouldn't survive in there.

Finally, he couldn't take it anymore. During lunch he talked with Andre about it in a place where no one could hear them. Immediately, he screamed quietly, venting quickly and with anger. "I can't take this anymore! This is the worst thing of all time! I can't believe this is happening to me! Ahh!" Andre quickly shushed him, and admitted that he had seen Max that day too, at the end of the day. Isaac calmed down, glad that someone else was there with him. They both decided that they had to do something, but for now they wanted to play it safe, even if they didn't want to. They wanted to explore, to see the world, to make everything crazy.

Isaac went home that day, angry but happy at the same time. He knew that he couldn't deal with Max, but he was also happy that he had Andre to help comfort him. He went to bed with him still at his side, and he was driven crazy by the taunts. They would never end. At least, that was what he thought. And his thoughts had been wrong a lot of times. In fact, he was incorrect almost all of the time.

Isaac turned over to his side, facing the wall. He did his best not to listen to Max's taunts as he continued to think about the search for knowledge. In science that day, they had talked about a curved universe. He wondered it that could add any possibility for time travel. Then, he wondered if he had the chance to travel back in time, he would, with all of the knowledge that he now had. He eventually decided that he wouldn't. Even if he skipped a bunch of grades, he would still be a social outsider. With that thought, he hoped that he could find someone to fill in for the old Max. Without him, he felt like something was missing in his life, like a puzzle that didn't contain a few of the pieces. It was unfinished, the image uncertain. However, he knew that no one could truly *replace* Max, so he dismissed this thought and flipped his pillow to the cold side, covering his ears with it, and soon he was fast asleep.

Chapter Thirteen

Choices

Isaac was in the middle of a mental catastrophe. Should he trust Andre? Should he not? Should he trust Holt? Should he share his thoughts with people? Who could he tell? All of these questions weighed his whole life down, driving him crazy. He was now at the boiling point, struggling to keep himself sane. He felt like someone was tearing his individual hairs out, one by one, and he could almost describe the sensation of each hair, the feeling of a searing pain, repeating over and over again.

He was surrounded by multiple copies of himself. He was in his normal bedroom, but his sheets were ruffled and he felt like he was going to die. Max was sitting on his bed, giving the usual taunts. He was used to it by now, but it still bothered him on the inside. He was just getting dressed, but a bunch of small copies of him were all around. They were staring directly into his eyes, following him as he walked around the room. One of them began speaking, saying, "Trust Andre! He'll be on your side." Another one was sitting next to him. "No! Don't trust him. He's working with Matt. He's a liar!"

They all began speaking at once, and no matter what Isaac could say or do there was no stopping them. They wouldn't stop, and he couldn't hear a single word of what they were saying. They all cut each other off, trying to get their point across. It didn't matter; he already knew what they wanted him to know. Some trusted Andre. Others didn't. Some trusted the other figure. Others didn't. He had heard it all before, except it was his own thoughts. While these were all still him, technically, they weren't at the same time. They were just figments of his own imagination, just like Max was, but they still made him question reality nonetheless. He wondered if he really was insane.

7:00. He immediately shot out of his bed and got dressed. He headed to the dining room, sitting down with his family, who were already there. They ate their crepes calmly, and they joked around quietly. Afterwards, they did what they always did: watch T.V. Of course, after a while, it was time to go to school, so that's what they did.

They climbed into their Toyota Hatchback and drove along, stopping along the way to pick up some paper. He wondered how long he could be able to see his parents.

They arrived at the school, and he entered alone. He was late. He headed to his locker, then to language arts, where his presence was questioned. He said that he had to stop for paper and he was sorry, then headed to his seat and worked on his book report, doing the best job that he could on it. He was required to make a poster about his book, and then write a speech about it. He was finishing the first phase, but it was hard to focus with Max taunting him in the background.

Eventually, Andre tapped him on the shoulder, asking, "So, what'd you dream?" Isaac replied by telling him every intricate detail, but not describing his feelings. He wasn't sure whether he completely trusted Andre yet, and he didn't want to accidentally reveal something that he shouldn't. Andre replied back by saying that he didn't quite know what to say, except for that maybe he was having a subconscious battle in his thoughts. His behavior and known knowledge would prove to tell who would win.

The next day, a Friday, Isaac woke up to the typical sound of Max's taunts. It was something that he was used to by now, even though he was bothered by it. He started to get dressed, but first decided to make his bed, hoping that it could help him make the dream less real. Max instantly sat down on the clean bed, ruffling the blankets and saying, "I know your thoughts. The dream will happen." The small people that were in his dreams started appearing in places everywhere in his room, from on the bed to his table. One of them even began to talk, and all of them followed suit, monkey see monkey do style. It was all the same, even the setting of the room that he was in. They were everywhere, and they drove him mad, making him want to stab himself in the ears to block out the noise, and then rip his eye sockets out like an avocado pit, because he didn't want to even see the smaller versions of him. It was no use; their words still crowded every thought in his brain, and during breakfast he struggled to hear and didn't utter many phrases. Eventually he arrived at school, and another figure appeared, saying, "You should tell Andre," and another, saying "No! Keep it all a secret."

Isaac decided to keep it a secret. In language arts, he kept his head down as he wrote his speech, but he didn't get much done. He was often being distracted by all of the voices in his head. He slumped in his desk at one point and asked to go to the bathroom. However, he didn't need to use it. He just needed a minute to himself. Later that day, at home, he took a shower, and whenever he dried off he imagined he was drying his old self off, beginning the transformation into a newer one.

That night, they went out to dinner, but he had trouble looking at the menu clearly. He gave up after a short amount of time and chose something randomly. About fifteen minutes later a grand bowl of tomato soup was brought to his table. He hated tomato soup. He let out a discreet and short sigh and ate it anyways, but he still struggled with it. He wasn't used to eating food he didn't like. His parents had recently been making only foods he enjoyed to eat. He wondered if they were worried about his safety as well, because they had been treating him with a lot of attention in the previous few weeks. He liked that extra attention, but it also unsettled him, like he was being shipped off somewhere that they, or he, didn't want to go. Of course, those questions just added to the amount figures around him.

The next day, finally the weekend, Isaac couldn't do anything that he wanted to do. In fact, he couldn't even focus on a single task. All of the small people in his mind had spiraled out of control, and their loud shouts began to hurt his ears. They were all trying to be more audible than the other one, to get their points across first. However, little did they realize that didn't matter, for they were all speaking at once.

At about 1:00 in the afternoon, Isaac's parents said that they would be going to the store. He chose not to come along, even though he liked to go to there routinely. Being in a public place in his mental state was something that he didn't want to do. Besides, the home alone time could almost give him some time to reflect. *Oh wait,* he thought, *I can't. These people stop me from doing so.*

As his parents closed the door and left, Isaac slumped down on the couch and tried to forget about the figures. It was no use; their noise drowned out everything else. He was driven mad by them, and nothing he could do would get him to forget about it. Still, he pressed on, trying to think of a solution. He had no idea what to do, and the figures kept getting louder and larger in numbers.

Finally, Isaac had an Idea. He looked over at all of the small people, and he thought long and hard about how they weren't real. They were just an illusion. He screamed at them, he shrieked at himself, and he even tried pinching himself for no apparent reason. Yet they were still there, louder than ever, and continuing to grow at an alarming rate. They were unstoppable, and Isaac gazed at them, feeling both hate and resentment towards them at the same time. He looked them dead in the eye, and finally he yelled, "You're not real! None of you are, so leave at once!" Nothing worked. They were still there, and they taunted him, along with a full-size version of Max.

Isaac looked at all of them again, and he had another idea. He forced his mind that he had made a decision of each of the things, and they slowly dissipated as he locked in his decisions for each thing. He secretly planned not to do them, but he figured that he could fool his conscious mind. They continued to disappear, and one even yelled, "No! I'm dying!" As it went back into his head. Finally, all of the figures were gone, and he saw Max slowly disappear as well, and eventually there were no figures left, and no Max, thank God.

Isaac's parents arrived home just as he sat down on the couch and turned on the television set. They asked him how it was at home, and he replied "quiet." It wasn't the most truthful answer, but what could he say? Plus, it was also an answer that sounded plausible. It wasn't a bad lie.

He asked his parents how their adventure at the store was, and according to them, it was 'exciting.' They all laughed and he helped his parents unpack the groceries. Later on that night he even assisted them in cooking, even though the dinner finally had something he didn't like: Brussels Sprouts. Finally, they had prepared and made something he hated. In fact, he would rather eat tomato soup than that. Still, at the dinner table he ate them without complaining, and he was rewarded with not having to do the dishes. Fine by him.

That night, Isaac stared up at the ceiling. He could finally sleep in peace. Just as he was about to doze off, he remembered that he would dream that night. He hated his dreams, but he still had to sleep. Before he slept, though, he turned to his side. He wondered if he really was crazy. He didn't seem like that, but he certainly felt it, to the point where he could kill himself. Of course, he wouldn't do that, but what was the point of living a life of fear and mystery? *I guess that's the fun of it,* he thought. That was what made life worth living; not knowing what was going to happen next. Living a life with every path laid out was boring. He wanted adventure; he wanted something to talk about at the water cooler at work someday. Of course, he didn't want an office job, and he was unsure of him even living to that point. He hoped that he could, although he wasn't sure. He still pressed on, fighting for his life. It was all a big mystery. Nothing seemed to make sense, and the things that did were small and vague in detail. There wasn't much to go by, yet there was so much question, a plethora of things to discover. They were all just hiding, somewhere stored away for civilization to find. Eventually they would, and Isaac hoped he would be around to see it. To him, humanity was entering a golden age, and he would quite literally trade the world to see it. While he wanted to be safe, he sought knowledge. He wanted to see the universe, to become one of the people, (or maybe even the sole person), to sculpt the scientific push for beyond the known universe. He had to be there to see it, and he would do almost anything to be a part of it. Maybe someday he could figure out the secrets of time travel, besides the clock, and he could go back in time to see Lucy.

Maybe things would look up, maybe they couldn't. Isaac would just have to wait and see.

Chapter Fourteen

Friends

All Isaac could see was an intense shade of pitch black. He peered to his left and his right, but he couldn't see anything besides darkness. He had no idea where he was, and his senses were cut off. He couldn't see, he couldn't hear, and he could hardly think. He was pretty sure that he was in another lucid dream, but he couldn't be certain. He was unsure of what to do, so he continued to stand where he was. He began to get paranoid, and a trickle of what he was sure was sweat slid down his face. He tried to look around once again, but there was nothing. He was alone, isolated from reality, and he was the universe, all at the same time. He could be anyone, anywhere, but he couldn't see it. He was blocked off from what there really was.

Isaac sat up. He glanced over at the clock, and as always it was 7:00 A.M. He looked around and smiled. There were no small versions of him, filling his ears with everything that he was thinking. There was also no Max, something he was happy about as he got dressed, once again heading to the dining room. Interestingly enough, his parent's weren't anywhere. He went back into the kitchen, and no one was cooking. There was no breakfast laid out, but there was a box of raisin bran on the counter. He walked over to it and noticed there was a note next to it, so he read it in his head.

Sorry, Isaac. I was called into work for an emergency surgery, and dad has early-morning jury duty. Things will return to normal tomorrow, but for now there's some cereal next to this note. In case if you've forgotten, the bowls are in the above cabinet, the spoons are in the below drawer, and the milk is in the fridge.
Love you,
Mom.

Isaac chuckled at the joke about the bowls, even though it wasn't that funny and he grabbed a cereal bowl from the cabinet. He thought about his mother's surgery. Even though she was a doctor, she didn't do many surgeries; she had just gotten certification six months ago. Still, this must have been important, if she was being called in as well.

The hospital must have needed everybody that they could get. He poured some cereal and milk in his bowl, grabbing a spoon and sitting down on the couch, just like old times. He placed his bowl on the coffee table and turned on the T.V. He tuned it to his new favorite show, *Hell's Kitchen.*

Just as he watched it, he realized that he had never planned a funeral for Lucy. The thought sat in the back of his mind as he watched the television screen. He eventually turned it off and worked on some weekend homework, (his math teacher was annoying like that), and he waited for his parents to arrive home.

Isaac's dad was at the door first. He knocked, and then he creaked it open slowly. He walked inside and placed his cup of Starbucks coffee on the kitchen table, sitting on the couch. He sat for a few more minutes, and finally Isaac asked him how the jury duty was. He replied by telling the whole story about it.

"Well, the case was really interesting! There were two people, one who claimed he owned a motorcycle, and another who claimed that the first one had stole it. They had used to be friends, but now they were actually at each other's throats. They hated each other! Anyways, as I was saying, there was evidence for and against both people, but long story short we chose the first person to be guilty. He got sentenced to a year and a half in prison! But, I'm talking about myself too much. How was home?"

"It was fine. I watched some T.V, and then worked on some math homework. Say... I have a question." Isaac replied.

"What?"

"Well," He beat around the bush a bit, worried what his dad would say. "We never had a funeral for Lucy, and I was wondering if we could, well, plan one."

"Oh my gosh, son! That reminds me, mom and I have been planning a funeral for her, slowly but surely."

"Really?" Isaac didn't say it aloud, but he wanted to be a part of planning that. It made him a little bit upset.

"Yeah. Actually, let me check my phone here..." His father pulled out his phone. "Let's see... calendar, upcoming events... oh! I don't know how to put this without sounding like I forgot the date, but apparently it's... well... in just a week. Next Sunday."

"What?"

"Yeah... say, you need a suit! Yeah, let's go and get you one."

All of this news was a surprise to Isaac. He was going to a funeral for Lucy, and it was in only a week? He was both offended and surprised that he wasn't involved in the planning, for he was her best friend, but he didn't say anything. He knew that his parents were just trying to do something nice for him, but it still bothered him that he didn't even hear about it. He inferred that they wanted to surprise him.

The men's formal wear store was enormous. It felt like a warehouse, but Isaac's dad said they had come there because "it was the cheapest store in town." That line had been said a thousand times before, and, really, it's said by everyone. After five minutes of searching, they finally found the teenagers section, but only with the help of a clerk. After another ten minutes, he found a great-looking outfit. It was a full set, coming with a black suit jacket, a white button-down undershirt, pants that matched the dark tone of the jacket, and, to top it all off, a wonderful red tie. He put it on in the dressing room and walked out, both feeling and looking more "snazzy" than he ever had. He almost felt like he was as rich as Donald Trump, although he was a brunette, and didn't have a crazy comb over. To make matters even better, the whole set was only two hundred dollars. His dad had been right; this store was extremely cheap.

Isaac and his dad arrived home shortly after buying the suit, and his mom was there as well. She had gotten a ride from a friend to work, he realized. They only had one car. He glanced over at a clock, noting that it was 2:00. They all immediately climbed into the family vehicle and headed up to the store. He roamed the isles, tasting samples as his parents bought their groceries, and at 2:45 they went home, finally finishing all their errands for the day. Mom said that the surgery went well; it was an emergency heart transplant, and they had needed all the hands they could get. The surgery was an overall success, and it was finished in only three and a half hours, a record time.

That night, after dinner and some more television, Isaac gazed up at his roof as he always did. He suddenly became terrified as he remembered the dream that he had. He had no idea what was going to happen, because all of his senses had been shut off. It was almost like someone had put earmuffs over his ears, and forced him to wear a blindfold. He wondered if that was what his dream would be, or if there was another reason for it. He took a long, deep sigh and went to sleep, knowing that he would have to be extremely cautious the next day.

Isaac woke up and looked around. He was still in his normal room, and he had woken up at just the right time, the same as always: 7:00 A.M. He climbed out of his bed and put on his clothes, wearing a sporty but comfortable neon yellow shirt and blackish-green shorts. He went to the kitchen and was happy to see that both of his parents were in the kitchen, working together to make breakfast. His dad was chopping the fruits and setting out the toppings, and his mom was cooking the actual crepes. He was happy by their group effort as he sat down in the dining room, eagerly watching as his dad laid out the various fruits. Eventually, his mom set the crepes down, and they all dug in, chatting and laughing. It was always an enjoyable experience.

At school, Isaac told Andre about the dream. He said that his senses were completely cut off, and Andre had no idea why that had happened, and he didn't have a dream that night. Isaac decided to be extremely cautious that day, and he said that he wouldn't trust anyone that he didn't know. He had no idea what the dream was, so he knew that anything could happen. He had to be prepared for it.

ARI LOHR

In language arts, it was speech day. Every student had to show off their poster and talk about their books, trying to get people to read it. While your grade was based on how good the actual project was, you could get extra credit for getting people to actually read the book. Both Isaac and Andre thought that it was a little bit unfair, but neither of them spoke up.

It was Andre's turn to speak. He walked over to the podium, but he didn't set any cards down on it. He had such a good memory that he could easily remember anything. He cleared his throat and had Isaac hold up his poster. He began to speak, talking in such a way where he could easily sell his book to an audience. Still, people in this high school were extremely biased, so nobody chose to read his book. In fact, someone even threw a wad of paper at him.

A few more people did their speeches, and then it was time for Isaac to have the floor. He stepped up to the podium and placed his cards on it. He had Andre hold up his poster, to a few boos as he spoke, doing even better then him. It didn't just surprise everybody watching, but it even surprised him. He wasn't used to giving good speeches. In fact, he was terrible at them. Every word that flew out of his mouth had an emotion,

138

but it was controlled. He was absolutely flawless, and his book was even interesting. It was about someone who dared to be themselves, and they ended up being super successful while most other people who had been rude to them failed miserably at life. Still, even with this great speech and good book topic, the whole time everybody could only see that Andre was his friend. Even though he was talented and polite, people now saw him as an outsider, an alien. He couldn't be trusted. At the end of the speech, everybody booed loudly, and they then threw even more wads of paper at him then as they did at Andre.

Derek stood up, and he looked around at the mess before him. People were throwing wads of paper and trash at one of his best friends, and not even the teacher was doing anything about it. He had to speak up, and he did. He cleared his throat and voiced his opinion. He scolded everybody who had been rude to Isaac and Andre, and the whole class glared at him, now seeing him as a symbol of hatred, someone not to be trusted. He said his final words and sat down, and the next person began their speech.

While it had been shrugged off in class, the news of the incident spread around the school as fast as a cheetah can run. By lunchtime, Isaac,

Andre and Derek were sitting alone, and everyone who walked by did something mean to them, be it smacking them on the head or hitting their lunch. Still, all three of them knew that it didn't matter, and Isaac went to sleep tonight knowing they were his only true friends, and he decided that he would tell Derek about the dreams the next day.

Chapter Fifteen

Assault

Derek had been Isaac's friend for two years. He was originally shy, but with the help of Isaac he was turned into someone who was extraordinarily outgoing, kind, and a great person overall. Originally, they didn't like each other, but whenever they got to know one another they became good friends. Derek had just moved to Arizona, and didn't know anybody in his new school. He didn't really talk to anyone, but he was forced to work with somebody whenever he was partnered up with Isaac for a science project. He was difficult to work with and didn't help out much, and he said almost nothing in their required presentation of the project. Because of his lack of helping out, they ended up getting a low "C" on the project, causing Isaac to dislike him.

Derek felt guilty about what had happened. He tried to talk to Isaac, but every time he was only turned away, unsure of what he needed to do next. He came back and demanded that his apology be accepted, but it wasn't. Nothing would make Isaac budge, and he tried to forget about the whole ordeal. He moved on with his life, a general dislike for his old partner. Isaac did the same thing, except he didn't like the other person, not himself.

Out of sheer luck, Derek was partnered up with Isaac again, this time for a social studies project. He tried to work with him, but Isaac didn't do anything. He tried apologizing to him again, but that didn't work. Eventually, he made it up to him by making him a card, (with a little piece of candy in the center), and he promised that he would work as hard as he could. This was a promise that he kept; he worked even harder then the person he was trying to apologize to, and he even spoke in the required speech, doing better than most kids who give speeches.

After the second project together, Isaac and Derek became best friends. The only person that Isaac liked more was Lucy. He had taught Derek how to be more outgoing and less shy, and Derek showed him his methods for studying. Just like Andre, he used to be shy, smart, and hate people. Even now, he was smarter than him, but he had no way near the intelligence of Andre. His intelligence wasn't at a school level, but rather at a cosmic level. He almost seemed to be all knowing, the most intelligent person on the planet. He was pretty much the next Albert Einstein, even though he was the opposite of the famous genius in his schooling years.

Isaac thought about all of this as he walked up to Derek, ready to tell him about the dreams. He was euphoric that the mystery dream had only resulted in a social climax, and nothing life-threatening. Still, it was bad to not have many true friends. At least he had Andre and Derek.

Derek was playing on his phone, and before school he came towards him, tapping him on the shoulder. He turned around to see Isaac, and he was a bit startled. "Hey." He said, smiling.

"Derek... there's something that I need to tell you."

"What?" Derek was now curious, but he had no idea of what was to come. He looked straight into Isaac's eyes and he laughed. Isaac wasn't laughing.

"Have you ever heard of a prophetic dream?"

"Yeah. Actually-they're pretty-"

"Great." Isaac cut Derek off, looking down at his feet as he spoke. "Well... I've been having them lately. A lot."

"Really?"

"Yeah. For about three weeks now, I have a dream, and then a day later it happens. Then, another day later, I have another dream. It's a vicious cycle!"

"Wow. Who have you told?"

Isaac didn't answer this question right away. "It doesn't stop there. Recently, the real life events have been a bit different than the dream, and just three days ago I had a dream where I couldn't see or hear anything, and I had no real idea what the dream was. I think it was the speech incident though."

"So, who have you told?" Derek replied.

"You and Andre. I tried to tell my parents, but they said that it was just a coincidence. They don't know the whole extent of it, though."

"So tell them."

"No! They already took me to a therapist, and she wants to send me to a mental institution. I love them, but I can't trust them with this."

"Well... I don't know what to say. I don't know anything about this subject."

"Can you keep it a secret?"

Derek looked Isaac in the eye, looking as trustworthy as possible. "Don't worry. I won't tell. I'll keep it as a secret, to my grave."

"Thanks, man."

With that, Isaac walked off, entering the school just as the bell rang. He went to his locker, and then directly to his first class of the day, language arts. It was speech day number two, as the class couldn't squeeze forty-three speeches in one day. Andre and Isaac sat down before the second bell rang, but they didn't say anything to each other. They decided to speak at lunch. Instead, they sat in the back of the class and watched politely as more people gave their speeches. None of them were as good as theirs.

Finally, after a couple more hours of different classes, it was time for lunch. Isaac walked into the lunch line and waited for it to move along. He chatted with Derek a bit, but they said nothing about the dreams. Saying it in such a crowded and public space would be a risk. So, they instead just made small talk, joking around. They talked about how stupid the speeches were, and most of them truly were. To avoid any conflict, they said only nice things about the people around them.

After about ten more minutes, (the lunch line was slow), Isaac and Derek sat down next to Andre. They didn't talk about the dreams, but whenever Derek excused himself to go to the bathroom, Andre immediately questioned Isaac.

"I saw you talking to Derek this morning. What was that about?"

"I told Derek about the dreams."

"What?!" Andre replied. He was furious. "You told him? This was supposed to be a secret between us. Us! Now that you've spread it to another person, you've expanded the probability for it being spread to even more people. You have no idea what you did, do you?"

Isaac felt terrible about what he had done. Andre was right; he leaked some of the information, and Derek could do anything with the knowledge. He could blackmail him, and he could do nothing about it. Still, he trusted him. He was his best friend! But, some of his other friends had betrayed him on speech day, so why wouldn't Derek?

Derek returned from the bathroom, and for the rest of the lunch period, it was only random chat, gossip, and jokes. Apparently, Joe, one of the people in language arts, had given the worst speech of all time. He walked up to the podium and didn't say a word. Instead, he just did his in interpretive dance. How do you turn a book into a one-man dance? Isaac thought. He asked the question, and everyone just shrugged. It was a mystery.

The bell rang, and Isaac, Derek and Andre said their goodbyes as they went to their classes. Sadly, none of them had the same classes for the rest of the day, So, Isaac was stuck being bored out of his mind, unsure of who to talk to or what to do.

After a few more hours of pure boredom and longing for friends, the bell rang for the end of the day, and Isaac sprinted out of his gym classroom, directly to his locker. He entered his locker combination and it opened, and he pulled out his backpack, slinging it over his shoulder. He didn't grab anything else, because he didn't have any homework, so he slammed the locker shut and realized that he had to go to the bathroom. He opened his locker and put his backpack back in it. He wasn't going to put it on the bathroom floor, and there were no shelves or hangers for it. He walked to the boys' bathroom and went inside. Standing on the other side was one of the burly teenagers from the detention, and he immediately tried to walk out, but he was pulled inside. The burly teen turned him around to face him, and Isaac struggled as he was pulled inside the bathroom. They were completely alone, and he let out a scream for Bloody Mary as a punch connected with his face. He knew that no one could hear him, because the walls of the school were well insulated, and he was punched in the stomach. He fell onto the ground and bent over, guarding his stomach as he was kicked in the shins. He quickly grabbed the teen's legs and pulled him town. The teen turned around as he looked at Isaac intently, and they were on each other in an instant, clawing and screaming as they tried to get the upper hand over each other. The larger teenager won, and Isaac was once again being kicked on the ground. The pain coursed through his body as he was punched, kicked, and stomped on, and he crawled towards the bathroom door. He reached his hand up and tried to open it, but he was immediately pulled back, just as he let out a scream.

The door swung open and a teacher walked in. He looked at both Isaac and the teenager, and immediately saw that he was covered in bruises. The other teen was fine, only with a couple minor scratches. The teacher said something into his microphone, and a few more teachers and faculty walked in. They pulled the teen out of the room and helped Isaac up. He was clearly in pain, but he was also in a daze, dizzy and almost unsure of what had happened. He had almost been knocked out, and he could have easily been beaten to death.

Isaac climbed into the family car and explained to his parents what had happened. He didn't want to, but he knew that the cuts and bruises easily gave him away, so instead of giving a lame excuse he came clean. His parents understood, and they all went out to dinner that night, at the same restaurant that he had accidentally ordered tomato soup at before. This time, he ordered a nice, juicy cheeseburger, and he thoroughly enjoyed it. Even though he had been beaten up, being able to go out with his family for a nice dinner was worth it; he loved his parents, and he didn't want to ever lose them.

That night, Isaac lay in his bed and stared at the wall in front of him. He was used to staring at the ceiling, but this time he felt more comfortable sleeping on his side. It helped ease the pain of the bruises on his stomach even more than all the ice packs that his parents had given him. He recapped the day, and he mentally scolded himself for how stupid he was for telling Derek about the dreams. He wished that he could travel back in time to stop it. If only he had that clock.

Isaac slammed his fist on the mattress below him. He could've used the clock to go back in time and save Lucy, but he didn't. He destroyed it as soon as he could, even though he could've had a plethora of knowledge with it. He could have seen the world, and he might have even had a chance to interpret the dreams, but he didn't. He got rid of his one advantage, the one weapon that he could use in his favor. He tried not to think about it anymore, because what was done was done. He worried about his dream some more, did a silent prayer to whatever god or almighty being was out there, and he prepared himself for the dream that was to come, finally falling asleep later on in the night.

Chapter Sixteen

Missing

Isaac woke up and glanced at his clock. Typical. It was 7:00 A.M, Friday morning. He climbed out of his bed and slipped on some clothes, wearing a light blue shirt and black pants. They weren't dress pants, but they still looked pretty fancy. He rushed downstairs, and his parents were there, making him crepes. He sat down by the dining room table, eagerly watching as they set out the toppings, and finally, the crepes themselves. He thanked them for making him breakfast and ate with them, talking up a storm. It was his favorite part of the day. Afterwards, they all watched T.V, and at about 7:35 they climbed into the family car once again.

Isaac knew something was wrong as soon as he got to Mears High. Andre wasn't standing out front, and whenever he looked through the school he was nowhere. With all the things that had been happening lately, anything that was out of the ordinary frightened him. So, whenever Andre was nowhere to be found, he immediately thought that Matt had something to do with it. Everything seemed to not make sense, but he was sure that it did it. He was positive.

Isaac trudged to his locker and opened it, putting his backpack in and pulling out his language arts binder, a pencil, and his vocabulary book. He walked into his first period of the day and looked around for Andre, who was nowhere to be found. He sat down and opened his vocabulary book, writing down the words in it. He knew that was what they were going to work on, and he was right; the teacher told them to open their books whenever the class started. He was happy that he got to work on it, because it was a great way to distract him from the real issue: Andre, and his dreams.

At lunch, Isaac talked with Derek some more about the dreams. He had already told him about them, but now he regretted it. He decided that he couldn't reverse what he had said, so he went the full mile, describing each dream, and, finally, Andre disappearing. They both wondered why he didn't have a dream the previous night, but the answer to that question was a mystery to them. They looked for Andre while they ate, but he was nowhere to be found. When the bell rang, they both gave up and headed back to class.

Isaac went through the rest of the day without much issue. Nobody threatened him, and he heard that the kid who had beaten him up got caught with a gun at school and was arrested. He was relieved to hear this news, but hearing that a student had tried to bring a weapon to school was unsettling. He thought about this as he rode home with his parents.

The next day, a Saturday, Isaac took a walk through the park. He watched some of the little kids playing and smiled warmly, and he took a lap around the play structure. He climbed up a tree, sitting on a branch for a few minutes, and then he climbed back down, looking at the tree again. There, right on the bark was a piece of paper, nailed into the tree.

Missing:
Andre Gonzalez.
Last seen 10/18/15,
10:00 P.M.
5,000 dollar reward for info leading to an arrest.

Isaac gawked at the piece of paper in despair. Andre wasn't just sick, and he wasn't responding to phone calls because he was busy. He was truly missing, and Isaac had a terrible feeling in his gut. He knew that Andre was probably with Matt, but he wasn't entirely sure. The kid who got arrested could have gotten him hurt, or worse. He shivered at this thought, and once again he thought about how he didn't have a dream the previous night. Did it all mean something? Did everything somehow add up to one big climax, and lead to a resolution, with either him or the unnamed antagonist winning? Was it all for a reason?

Isaac sat up and looked at his clock. 7:00. He checked his phone, and it was Friday. It really was a dream. He sprinted to the kitchen to see his parents cooking crepes once again, and he ate them with them. Afterwards he watched television with them, as he always did, finally heading out to school. At approximately 7:50, he arrived at Mears High, and he left the car. He immediately searched for Andre, who was nowhere to be found. He frantically continued to look, and he ran into Derek. He told him about his dream, and they both looked for Andre until the bell rang, afterwards heading their separate ways, eventually meeting up in language arts class. Once again, Andre was nowhere to be found, and they both desperately searched for him whenever and wherever they could.

At lunch, Isaac met up with Derek again, and they both looked for Andre together. They looked throughout the whole school but he was nowhere, so they headed off campus, searching in local businesses and restaurants. Unless something bad had happened or he was sick, he was eating lunch somewhere. He tried to call and text him on his phone, but he didn't answer the calls or reply to the texts. Instead, he remained silent and missing, and no one had any idea where he was.

The rest of the day went by normally, but Isaac was still unsure of Andre's location. He couldn't find him anywhere, but he still continued to search. However, his efforts were unsuccessful. That night, he gazed up at his ceiling, thinking about the dream. He knew what he would do the next day.

It was a cool and crisp Saturday morning. Isaac got up and made himself some breakfast, turning the T.V on. As soon as his parents came downstairs and had their coffee, he said that he was going to the park, which they allowed him to do. He immediately rushed out the door, sprinting to the park. He ran to the tree that was in his dream. There it was, and he saw that the missing poster was there. He climbed up the tree and sat down, heaving a long and frustrated sigh. He was able to do something about most of the dreams, but in this one he couldn't. Andre was probably in the arms of Matt, and he couldn't do a single thing about it, unless if he saw Matt, which was probably not going happen.

Isaac went home after a few more minutes, and he lied in his bed, staring up at the ceiling like he always did. He wondered where Andre was, and he knew that he had no chance of finding him. He continued to search around local areas, with a little bit of help from his parents, (he had only told them about Andre being missing, nothing else), but there were no positive results. Whoever had taken Andre had covered up their tracks very well.

Sunday.

It had been another day, and it was the date of Lucy's funeral. Isaac got up and headed downstairs, pouring himself some cereal. After he ate it, he put on his expensive suit and watched some T.V, being careful not to damage the suit. After a while his parents came downstairs, and they all headed to the graveyard together.

Once they arrived at the graveyard, they remained fixated at the hole that had been dug for Lucy. There was a large tombstone over it, but it was a tiny, but deep, hole. Lucy had been too mangled to just put in a coffin and bury, so her parents had opted for cremation instead. He was glad that he didn't have to see the cremation, but he was still upset that his parents didn't ask him if he was okay with seeing it. They just assumed whether or not he had wanted to do something.

They were about ten minutes early, so they waited as more people showed up, and finally, after twenty more minutes, a priest came with Lucy's ashes. Isaac and his parents weren't Christian, but Lucy and her family were, so it was a religious ceremony, and she was buried with a cross around her ash box. Isaac watched as more and more people came by, and after about a half an hour after his family showed up the service started.

"We are all gathered here today to honor and mourn the death of Lucy Glaskow. She was considered a great woman by many, and to others she was considered someone who was learning how to sprout and become one. To me, she was an excellent student and a good friend... and this death has hurt me as well. We would like to have one last church service for her before she is buried, and then we'll have people say a few words about her if they would like. Finally, her ashes will be buried underground, and we will have a small lunch together before heading home. So, with that being said I would like to begin the church service with a song. Please, all rise from your seats to sing with us. If you don't know the song, or would like to just follow along, it's on page 445 of your bibles." The priest spoke slowly and solemnly, and Isaac could tell that he was trying not to burst into tears.

The church service went on for two hours. It was prolonged to honor Lucy, so Isaac was left being both despondent and bored by the end of it. He didn't want to see her buried, and he wasn't ready to let go, but he knew that he would have to. Finally, after 120 minutes of the priest speaking, it was time for people to speak their final words. The priest asked if anybody would like to say their thoughts and, and Isaac immediately raised his hand, being ushered to the podium.

"I would first like to say that Lucy was a good friend to me... and I'm sure that her sudden death was a surprise to both me, and all of you people here today." Isaac wiped a few tears off his face and continued. "She was my best friend, and I feel terrible for losing her. Sadly, I had to, and I would like to say a few things to her before she gets buried." He turned towards the box containing Lucy's ashes. "Lucy, I'm sorry for all of the fights that we ever had. You were the world to me, and your death has brought despair on me, and among all of the people here today. The car that had hit you hasn't been brought to justice just yet, but instead it's done more and more crimes. The police are currently looking for it, yet, nobody has noticed the license plate number yet. I would like to finish up by saying that you were a great person, and let God have mercy on your soul... amen." With that, Isaac stepped down from the podium and back to his seat.

A few more people spoke about Lucy and her death, and after that it was finally time to bury her. The priest and a few other people dressed in white robes blessed her, and then her box was lowered into the hole. The hole was filled with the dirt that had been dug up earlier, and lunch was served. Isaac made a sandwich with the deli placed out, and he didn't say a word to anybody as he ate. He just gazed directly at Lucy's tomb stone, and a few tears slid down his cheek. He did his best to fight his tears in this public place, and he was lucky to know that fighting them back worked; he didn't cry that much.

That night, as Isaac tried to sleep, he thought about his whole adventure. Lucy's death, talking to Andre, the pyramid figure, coming out to Derek about the dreams, and now, Andre being missing. He wished that he could go back in time and do something about his disappearance, but he knew that that wish would never come true. Still, he thought, anything can happen. That was his last thought of the night, and a few minutes later he fell into a silent and dreamless sleep.

Chapter Seventeen

Escape

Isaac sat up without looking at his clock and put his clothes. He wore a red shirt and blue jeans, the same outfit he had worn the day before Lucy got ran over. He rushed downstairs to the kitchen, and he saw his parents making crepes. They had done that ever since he had gone to the therapist. He sat down in the dining room, and he waited for his parents to lay out the toppings, and finally, the crepes themselves. After a few minutes, all of the toppings and crepes had been laid down, and he and his family were ready to eat their food. They ate and talked up a storm like they always did, and afterwards they watched T.V. Finally, it was time to leave to go off to school, and he wished that it wasn't a Monday.

At school, Andre was nowhere to be found. He had been missing for a few days, and he was still gone. The police hadn't questioned Isaac and his family yet, but he knew that it was coming. He chatted with Derek about Andre being gone, and then he headed inside the school. He went to his locker and spun the combination, and the first bell rang as he put in his backpack and pulled out his language arts binder, a pencil, and his vocabulary book as always. He walked to class with him, and he was glad that they sat near each other.

The teacher told them to pull out a piece of paper and a pencil, so they did. The headed it with their names, period number, and the date, and they were told to number their papers from one to ten. They numbered their papers, and then they were told that this was a quiz. *A pop quiz?* Isaac thought. *On a Monday?* He sighed in frustration as he continued to listen to his teacher. She said that she was going to ask them ten questions, and they had to write down the answer on their pieces of paper. The teacher asked them the first question.

"What are the three basic principles of good storytelling?" The teacher asked. Isaac was immediately confused. They had never learned this. *Plot, characters* and *development,* he wrote on paper, but he really had no idea what it was. The teacher asked the next question. "Which of these statements are correct: Tommy walked to the bathroom? Or, Tommy had walked to the bathroom?" Isaac thought that both of these were correct, but he wasn't sure if that was a valid answer. After a minute of consideration, he wrote down that both of them were correct.

It went on like this for five more minutes, and then the teacher read off the answers. Isaac got most of them incorrect, but he could tell that most other people did as well. Derek got a perfect score, but he always did. Andre probably would've as well. However, Isaac was still confused. They had never learned this material! The teacher collected all of the papers, and she eyeballed every single student. Most of them were concerned about their scores, and right as someone was about to cry, she finally spilled the beans. "Well, class, I have a little secret to reveal. This was a pretest." The whole class heaved a long and peaceful sigh, and the teacher taught them the new unit. It was actually quite easy.

Isaac ended up not having any more quizzes or tests to do that day, much to his relief. The whole day had been a breeze, which was great. It was an easy Monday. Still, he thought about Andre's location. Was he even alive? He wondered this as he walked around, deciding to ask his parents to do another search around the neighborhood. The declined it, saying that it was too dark outside to find anything. That was true, since the sun had set a bit earlier that day. Instead, they ate tacos for dinner, and afterwards they watched television. They ended up watching reruns of *Saturday Night Live*, and finally, at 10:00, he went off to bed.

Isaac gazed up at the ceiling, and he tried to go to sleep. He wanted to get the dream over with, but he was unsure of what to expect. One of the last dreams he had was blocked off, so he wondered whether he would be able to see it or not. He hoped that he would come across Andre, but he knew that he wouldn't. Still, he remained hopeful as he dozed off to sleep, ready but not at the same time to see a fragment of his future.

Darkness. Isaac was surrounded completely by another intense shade of pitch black, just like the dream that he had a few days ago. He looked around him, but he could clearly see nothing. He tried to listen for a sound, but there was none. He moved his arms around, be he quickly realized that he couldn't; his hands were bound by ropes. A trickle of sweat streamed down his face, and he immediately tried to get out of the ropes that trapped his hands. They began to go numb, and he realized just how tight they were. He kept on trying to break free, but it was no use; he was trapped. He scrunched his face at the strain of being held up by the ropes, similar to how he acted whenever he was kidnapped. Suddenly, he found out another thing. His eyes were covered with a blindfold. He began to panic. Someone, or some*thing* had kidnapped him, and they blocked out his senses. He continued to tug at his bounds, but he eventually gave up, hanging in pain and despair.

Isaac woke up, looking around. He was comforted to see that it was his own room, but he was also disturbed at the dream that he had. He had been kidnapped again, and he had to be careful on Wednesday. For now, however, he climbed out of his bed, glancing at his clock. It was 7:00 in the morning. He put on the first clothes that he saw, another red shirt with an *Under Armor* logo on it, and white pants. They looked neither flashy nor stagnant. They were just in between, on the edge, like Isaac's mind was. He headed downstairs and immediately headed to the dining room, and he eventually ate more crepes with his parents. Afterwards he watched T.V with them, and whenever the time was right they all headed to school in the same Toyota Hatchback as always.

Andre was nowhere to be seen, and Isaac was still terrified. He ignored the thought and walked to his locker, grabbing his stuff and heading off to class. There, he and his peers continued to learn their new unit, how to write a good story, and he excelled at the activity that they had to do. He wasn't as good as Derek, but he was still proud of himself at what he had done. He went through the rest of the day euphoric, but he was immediately upset whenever he got home. He thought about Andre again, wishing that he could have done something to help with him getting kidnapped, but he knew that there was nothing he could do.

Just as he had this thought, Isaac's phone vibrated, and he reached into his pocket, pulling it out. He turned it on, and noticed that he had a new text message.

It was from Andre.

Isaac immediately opened the text. He was unsure of what to think, so he just read it quickly but carefully. *Isaac! I don't have much time to speak, but I can say that I've escaped from Matt. I don't know much, but he's coming for you next! You don't have much time. Hide yourself, quickly!* Isaac immediately freaked out, but he did his best not to make any noise. He tried not to attract his parents' attention, because they would ask what was wrong, and he would be in a tough spot.

The next day, Isaac did his best to watch the world around him, trying not to attract any attention to himself. He ate breakfast with his parents and watched television, but he still didn't let his guard down. He eventually made it to school, and he felt safe. *So far, so good*, he thought. He blended in with the crowd, and he saw Andre. He immediately ran towards him, and they hugged each other awkwardly. The moment ended quickly, though and Andre began to speak. "Good. Stay in a public area. He won't attack you here." Isaac had nothing to say to respond, but the bell rang anyways. He later met him in language arts class, and he helped him get accustomed to the new unit. He immediately exceeded at it, leaving Isaac in his dust.

Finally, the last bell of the day rang, and Isaac did his best to head to his parents' car slowly and quietly. He didn't want to attract attention, and he wanted to stall his time as much as possible. He entered the vehicle ten minutes late, and whenever they left, his parents told him that they were going on a dinner date. He would be left alone for a few hours during the night.

Isaac was horrified at the situation. He was going to have to spend the night alone, and he knew that he was going to get kidnapped. It was only a matter of time before he would be. He made himself some frozen pizza, and he sat on the couch and watched T.V. He made sure to lock his doors and draw the curtains, but he tried to relax a little bit. It was inevitable; he was going to be kidnapped. The question was, *who* would take him hostage? Would it be a human, or would it be Matt, or possibly another out-of-this-world body? He would have to wait to find out.

The time was 7:30 P.M, and Isaac was still in his house. He had finished his pizza and washed his dishes, but he was still tense about what was going to happen. He tried not to think about it, but that was impossible. How could somebody forget that they were inevitably going to be kidnapped? The thought wasn't always in his conscious mind, but it was somewhere in the back of his mind. It darkened his overall mood, but after a while, he began to question the dream. It was 9:00, and he still hadn't been kidnapped, or even attacked. He began to wonder if the dream's information was truly credible, but he assumed that it was. They had never failed him, which was probably a bad thing.

The clock read 10:00 P.M, so Isaac went off to bed. He did his best to go to sleep, and he was happy to know that both the dream and Andre had been incorrect. He was finally going to be safe! He covered his head with the blankets, but it was only for comfort. He happily went off to sleep, and he didn't have a single dream.

Isaac woke up a few hours later, but it was too dark to see. He tried to glance over at his clock, but he could barely move his neck. His head was sore, and he tried to massage it with his arms. He attempted to reach it with them, but they were bound.

The dream had come true! Isaac had let his guard down, and now he was stuck in a place that was unfamiliar to him. He had no idea of his location, because his eyes were covered with a blindfold, once again just like in his dream. He started to cry, but he held most of the tears in. He was both afraid and furious at himself, and he knew that he was probably going to be hurt, or worse.

He was going to be killed.

Isaac did a short prayer to a nameless god that he wasn't sure of its existence, and he did his best to stay alert. Finally, after a few more hours, he heard a door open, and he braced himself for what was to come.

Chapter Eighteen

Words

Isaac tried to look at the door that had just opened, but he couldn't see who had walked through. It was too dark to see, and he realized that he had a blindfold on. Once again, he tugged at the ropes holding his hands tight, but he couldn't escape. He let out a wail that was barely audible. It would have been louder, but it was mixed with the sound of him crying. He tried once again to pull the ropes loose, but he eventually gave up and cringed, waiting for whoever had walked through the door to hurt him.

After a few minutes, Isaac began to get confused. Someone had walked through the door, but where was that person now? He kicked in front of him, waiting to see if his legs would touch anything, but they just flew in the air. He tried to work his blindfold off, but it was tied tightly to his head. Without the assistance of his hands, he was going to have to be without vision. He stopped trying to get his blindfold off and hung midair, once again cringing. He was being played with, and he had to show that it wasn't affecting him.

Isaac waited patiently and quietly. He knew that he was probably not going to have another quiet moment, so he sat perfectly still, enjoying his last minute of peace. He knew that he was not going to have a dream that night, so he smirked a bit. He waited some more, and finally he heard a noise. It sounded like a ball, bouncing against a wall, repeating over and over again. He looked out in front of him, towards the source of the noise, but once again he realized that he was blindfolded. Instead, he remained silent as listened to the noise. It was repeating at a strict pace, never stopping, constantly making the same sound of hitting the wall. He guessed that it was about fifteen feet away from him, and that helped him estimate the area of the room. Still, he didn't know the width of it, so he didn't know exactly how large it was.

All of a sudden, a familiar voice ringed inside Isaac's head. "Hello, Isaac." "Andre?" He replied back, unsure of what else to say. "Yeah, Isaac, it's me."

Isaac was in complete shock. Andre had something to do with his kidnapping! He had no idea what to say, so he remained quiet, not uttering a single word. The room remained like this for what seemed like forever, and then Andre ended the awkward and tense silence. "Listen to me. I don't have much time at all." His speaking pace quickened. "Listen, I'm being forced to kidnap you, and you must make sure to-" There was a muffling noise, and a deafening scream was let out from his mouth. After thirty seconds, the room was silent, and Isaac cringed again, preparing for what was to come towards him next. He had no idea what it would be, but he knew that his friend was in trouble, so he might be as well.

The door slammed shut, and there was no noise inside the room. Isaac tried his best not to show any reaction to what had happened. Something might still be listening to him or watching him. He waited for something to happen, but nothing did. His breathing was quick and shallow, and he was terrified. He continued to wait, but after hours, he was still left without any indication of where he was, or what was happening.

Finally, the door opened again. Isaac's blindfold was taken off of him, and the whole room was blurry. To his right was a gray wall, and to his left was the same thing. On the ground was another drab floor. All were made of concrete. He couldn't see in front of him, because a harrowing and enormous figure stood in his view.

Matt.

Isaac was horrified, but he wasn't surprised. He had been attacked by Matt a lot recently, but he was confused. He could've been easily killed before, so why not? He knew that there was an important reason, and he knew that he could use that to his advantage. Before he could think anything else, Matt cut off his thoughts, speaking to him. "ISAAC! I'M SURE THAT YOU'VE MISSED ME! WELL, I HAVE SOMETHING BIG TO TELL YOU. WANNA KNOW WHAT IT IS?"

Isaac was startled, but he didn't want to show that to Matt. He remained silent and gazed deep into its eyes, doing his best to keep a straight face. "SPEAK TO ME, DAMMIT!" He still remained without a word, something that angered it even more. "IF YOU DON'T SPEAK TO ME," it held up a sharp knife, and a fiery passion burned in his eyes, "THEN I WILL DRIVE THIS KNIFE RIGHT THROUGH YOUR HEART!" Isaac knew that this wouldn't happen, and he still didn't speak as he was stared at. After a minute of this, Matt set down the knife, and he knew that he had an advantage. He could've easily been murdered, but he wasn't. There was a reason for that, and even if he didn't know it, he was important in some way. He would have spoke to it, but he was worried that he might give some information away that it needed. Finally, it spoke again. "FINE THEN. I'LL JUST TELL YOU. ANDRE, WELL, HE'S DEAD. I KILLED HIM, WITH THE VERY KNIFE THAT IS ON THE FLOOR NOW. I WOULD'VE KILLED HIM WITH MY MAGICAL POWERS, BUT I WANTED HIM TO SUFFER."

Isaac was despondent. One of his true friends, his source of information, had been murdered. He tried to remain strong, but a stream of tears quickly glided down his face, and he bawled loudly. Still, he didn't say a single word. "YUP. HE'S A GONER, AND IT'S ALL BECAUSE OF ME. ME!" Finally, Isaac couldn't hold himself back, and he began to yell as loudly as he could, still crying. "Why do you have to torment me? I'm just trying to live my life, but you have to constantly torment me and Andre!"

Before he could speak again, Matt began to shrink in size, and it was just as large as his mouth as it entered whenever he spoke. He tried to stop it, but he was too late, and his head began to ache. He tried to remain clear and coherent, but soon, everything fell black.

Isaac woke up in his room, looking over at his clock. It was 7:00 A.M, and he checked his phone. It was still Wednesday, but it was the morning again. Bewildered, he went downstairs and into the kitchen, seeing his parents cooking crepes again. He walked to the dining room and patiently waited, and finally his parents laid out all of the toppings for the crepes, and then the stars of the dish themselves. They sat down, and Isaac tried to say thank you to them.

"F*** you."

Isaac immediately covered his mouth with his hands. He didn't mean to say that, but that was what had come out of his mouth. His parents looked at him like he was crazy, and his mom told him to drop and do twenty push-ups for his rude behavior. He didn't say a word, but instead he did what he was told to do. It was the least that he could do for accidentally saying such a profane phrase. Afterwards, they ate their breakfast without speaking, and then they watched television. Isaac tried to say I'm sorry after that activity.

"You are the worst people ever."

Isaac shook his head and covered his mouth, wide eyed. Once again, something that he didn't mean to say had come out of his mouth. He decided to keep it shut, and his parents instantly drove him off to school. He was dropped off without a goodbye, and he looked for Andre. He couldn't find him, and he wondered if he was killed. However, he saw Derek, and the thought of Andre immediately left his mind. He walked over and said hi.

"I hope you die in hell fire."

What? Three times now, Isaac had said what he didn't mean to say. He tried to write down what he wanted to say in paper, but his hand didn't write what his brain had been thinking. He wrote another rude and profane thing, instead of what he wanted to write. He walked inside the school without another word, and as the bell rang he went to his locker.

It had been four periods, and Isaac had managed not to say a single word. He did his best not to speak, but inevitably he had to write on paper. Sadly, he didn't write what he wanted to. He wrote more rude things. In fifth period, the period that it was currently, he was in History. He was going to remain silent, but then his teacher said that she was going to randomly pick somebody to answer the questions. She asked the first question. "What is nine plus ten?" She picked a student, who jokingly answered "twenty-one," and the class laughed. The teacher also giggled, saying that that was a "joke".

The teacher randomly drew a name out of a jar full of Popsicle sticks. "Isaac," she said, and his heart dropped. He knew that if he said a word, he would immediately get in trouble, and he risked being suspended. He waited patiently for the question, and he didn't say anything out loud. "Okay, Isaac. What was the fashion for women in Imperial Japan?" He knew the answer, but he couldn't muster a word. The teacher and the rest of the class looked at him, waiting, and she asked him the question again. Finally, after a couple minutes, he had no choice but to answer it.

"Well, they looked ugly, kind of like you, little b****."

The teacher looked at Isaac like he was the devil himself, and she immediately sent him to the principal's office. The whole class was silent as he slowly trudged out, but whenever the door closed and he left, there was a cacophony of the room laughing, including the teacher. Isaac walked to the principal's office, and whenever she asked him what he had done wrong, he pointed at his mouth. She questioned what he meant, and he had no choice but to speak again.

"I got in trouble because my teacher is a little b****, just like you and your mother."

The principal let out a troubled gasp, and she called Isaac's parents. A few minutes later, they arrived, taking him home. He wished that he could tell them it wasn't his fault, but he knew he couldn't, so instead he just kept his mouth shut. Whenever he got home, he was sent to bed without dinner, just like a toddler would be.

In bed, Isaac gazed up at his ceiling, wondering what had gone wrong. He knew that his words were being controlled somehow, but he didn't know who, or what was doing it. He thought about any clues that he had, and then it became obvious.

Matt.

Isaac slapped himself in the face, and inside his head he yelled for Matt to get out. Surprisingly, he was met with a reply, which actually came with a whisper out of his mouth. "No. Andre is dead, and before I kill you, I'm going to make your life miserable. By the time I'm done with you, you'll be begging for death."

That was all Isaac needed to hear. He didn't say or think another word, and he quietly wept himself to sleep, knowing that there was truly nothing he could do. If only he could kill Matt, make it die. Then, maybe all of this would be sorted out. Still, he was at an extremely major disadvantage. Andre was dead, as far as he knew, and he couldn't tell anybody about his troubles. He stopped with that thought, and after a few more minutes of tossing and turning, he finally went to sleep for the night, unsure of what was to come later on.

Chapter Nineteen

Vacation

Isaac sat on his front porch, staring into an empty void. He didn't say a word, but rather he just gazed out, wishing for a way to kill Matt. He knew that it was important, and maybe if he killed it, he would have the key to stopping the dreams. Maybe it controlled the dreams. He really had no clue, so for now he just sat, thinking about Andre. He knew that he was dead, and he wondered it he was being looked down upon from a higher place, a source of Nirvana. He wanted to make a shrine or a tombstone to honor him, but he knew that if he was caught his parents would question him, which would result in him getting in even more trouble. Still, Andre was worth it, so he changed his mind and walked inside.

Isaac spent the next hour and a half making a clay tombstone for Andre. He first molded the shape of the tombstone, making sure that it was perfect, and then he used a fine knife to carve Andre's name into the clay.

Andre Gonzalez
Born: 4/6/2000
Died: 11/25/15
The key to the cosmos

Tears streamed down Isaac's face as he engraved to words, but he still kept going. His eyes stung worse than someone cutting an onion for the first time, but he fought his emotions and engraved, trying not to think about Matt. Still, he was constantly being bombarded by it, but this time he couldn't shout that it wasn't real. He had already tried blocking out his mind, but that didn't work. So, he did his best to forget about the constant taunts bothering him as he wrote.

Finally, Isaac had engraved the whole thing. He lay on his bed and glanced at his clock. 8:30. He would usually be in school that day, but because of his profanity he was suspended for the rest of the week. His parents were furious with him, but because he had never suspended before they were lenient. Still, they were visibly upset at him.

Just as he thought about this, his door creaked open, and his parents walked in. They looked into his eyes for a few seconds, and he looked into theirs, seeing tears. He turned away and didn't speak as his mother walked towards him. She told him that they were going on a trip for the weekend, and he would've asked where they were going, but he obviously couldn't. Instead, he just nodded his head, and his question was answered for him anyway. "I'm surprised you don't wanna know where you're, err, we're going. Do you?" Isaac nodded his head, and his mom replied to him. "We're going to Utah for the weekend, since dad received plane tickets for free from work. I hope you're excited."

Isaac smiled and nodded his head, and his parents looked at him for another few seconds, then turning and walking out of the room. Before his dad left, he turned back around to him and hesitated for a moment. Then, he spoke. "We're leaving for the airport at 3:30 in the morning tomorrow. Stupid flight schedules... he he. Anyways, have your stuff packed by then. I love you, son." With that, his dad walked out, and Isaac reached underneath his bed for his backpack. He unzipped the zipper and put a few sets of clothes inside. He also packed a water bottle on the side, and he stuffed his electronics on top of his clothes for easy access on the plane. He decided that he would charge his phone the night before. He also put his chargers, except for the one for his phone, into the bag. He thought about packing a knife in case he needed to defend himself, but he remembered that the TSA wouldn't allow that, so he put it back in the kitchen.

Later that day, Isaac sat on the couch, watching television, and his parents asked him what he wanted for dinner. For a second he struggled, because he couldn't speak or write properly, so he just shrugged. His parents exchanged glances for a second, and then they looked back at him. They said that they would pick, and they left to go to the store. An hour later, they returned with a fresh salmon, some fruit, some more cereal for breakfast, and snacks for the plane. The snacks consisted of chips, crackers, and gummy worms. He loved gummy worms.

At the dinner table, everybody ate their food without a word. Finally, his parents asked Isaac the deciding question. "Why?" His mother asked. "Why did you act so mean to people yesterday." He remained silent, and his parents looked at him, their piercing gaze penetrating through his body. He continued to be silent, and he opened his mouth to eat another piece of salmon.

"I see things! Things that you couldn't imagine. I have these dreams, and they all happen for real. Matt is coming to get me!"

Isaac swiftly covered his mouth. He didn't mean to say that, but Matt had forced him to. His parents exchanged glances once again, and his mother looked at him. "Who's Matt?" He remained quiet, but his parents looked at him, settling into their seats. They were willing to wait all night for an answer. He had no choice but to open his mouth.

"Matt is a flying pyramid. He haunts my dreams, and he also comes to hurt me in real life. Why, he's the reason why Andre's dead!"

"Andre's dead?"

"Yeah. Matt killed him, and he's going to enslave the whole world. He is the real God. He is the real Satan."

His parents didn't say another word, but he was sent to his room without words. That night, he looked up at his ceiling, thinking about what would happen to him. He was going on a trip to Utah, but would he be sent to a mental institution after the trip? He didn't know what would happen, so he decided to stay awake and alert in the coming days.

The next day, a Friday, Isaac woke up tired, cranky, and groggy. He forgot about Matt for a minute, and he opened his mouth to yawn.

"F***."

He stopped for a second and listened. He waited to be punished, but his parents hadn't heard it. He mentally scolded himself for forgetting about Tad, and he went downstairs to get some breakfast. He walked to the kitchen and grabbed a bowl, pouring the last of the old cereal box in it. He also finished the milk that day. He pulled a spoon out of one of the kitchen drawers, and then he sat down by the coffee table, eating it. He didn't watch T.V. Instead, he was courteous of his parents, being as quiet and discreet as he could. He checked his backpack to make sure he had everything that he needed for the trip after he finished his cereal, and then he sat back down on the couch. He was about to yawn again, but he caught himself at the very last minute, swallowing it just in time.

After a few more minutes, Isaac's parents walked down with their supplies, looking as exhausted as he did, and they all used the bathroom for the very last time. Isaac went as quickly as he could, excited for the trip. Little did he know that might have been the last time he used the bathroom in his own house. The family climbed into their car. Isaac had a great feeling in his gut, which only fueled his excitement for the trip that he was about to have.

Isaac hadn't ever been on an airplane before. One time, his family was about to go, because his parents had won free tickets from a raffle, and everyone was excited to go the Bahamas. He was eight at the time, and he didn't know that he wasn't allowed to bring weapons on planes. He had this dream of cutting coconuts off the tops of trees, (something that his parents would never let him do), so he put a pocket knife in the middle of his bag. He placed it there in the middle because he wanted it to remain "safe," whatever that means. However, to an eight year old, that might be a plausible option. Whenever they got to the airport, they walked in, and his parents printed out their tickets. They waited in line for the TSA screenings, and finally, after thirty minutes, they had gotten to the front of the line. He placed his backpack on the conveyor belt and watched it slowly move across, finally going underneath the scanner. There was a deafening beeping sound, and he and his family were rushed to a small room. It was for interrogations. After an hour of being questioned by the FBI, he and his parents were free to go, but they had missed their flight.

That brought them to now. Before they had left, his parents checked his backpack, just in case, and they were off, driving in the car. It took an hour, but the vehicle finally stopped. However, there was something interesting. They weren't at an airport.

They were at a mental institution.

Isaac and his parents walked inside, and they were inside a small lobby. There was a desk with a receptionist, and his parents talked to her for a minute, finally releasing him to her. They both hugged him, in tears, saying that they loved him. They walked out the door, but before they did, his dad turned around for the very last time. "Son, this decision was almost impossible for us. We weren't going to do this, but how you've acted lately, not just the rude comments, and what you said the other day... it all adds up. I'm sorry that it had to add up to this, but this was all that we could do. I love you."

Isaac knew that they weren't doing all they could do. Anger stormed through his body as he was taken to another room. This one had multiple chairs laid out in a circle. People in plain white clothes were sitting in them, but one of the chairs was covered by someone who wore regular clothing. They had a large clipboard, and it wasn't exactly clear whether they were a boy or a girl. Isaac was taken to the last vacant seat, and he sat down as the receptionist walked out of the room, closing the door behind her.

Nobody said a word as they all sat around. The other person, whom he guessed was a therapist, wrote something on their clipboard. They looked at him, and then they looked back down at their clipboard, continuing to write, but now quickening their pace. The silence drove him crazy, but he didn't open his mouth. His mind began to wander to stupid topics, and he wondered what he would do if he had a cold. He silently chuckled to himself as he thought about this, but the humor ended quickly. He was in a mental institution! He did his best to keep calm on the outside, and he looked like he was. However, on the inside, he was in a panic. He had no idea what he was going to do. He wasn't crazy, he was normal!

Right?

Maybe Isaac was insane. Maybe everything had been a part of his imagination. Maybe he had schizophrenia. He knew that it was weird to think about, but people with that mental disorder don't know they have it until they're diagnosed. Sweat began to bead on his forehead, and he wondered if he actually was normal. There was no real way to know, so he didn't rule out the possibility. He almost hoped that he was crazy, just to know that it was all a figment of his imagination.

Isaac's thoughts were cut off as the therapist spoke quietly, putting down their clipboard. "Hey, everybody. You all know me, but we have a new guest today, Isaac Crowley."

Chapter Twenty

Insanity

Isaac listened quietly and attentively as the person spoke. He still wasn't sure whether they were a man or a woman, but it would be rude to ask. He hoped they would tell him soon. He sat around in a circle, looking around as he/she spoke. "Isaac, my name's Donna. Donna Wilkins. Now, you may be wondering why you're here. Would you like to explain it, class?" The whole group besides Isaac responded in unison, sounding monotone, like robots. "Because some people need a little push in the right direction." He also noticed that they gritted their teeth while saying it, and he inferred they didn't like it in this place. The therapist continued speaking. "Isaac, this circle is a community. Here, you can feel free to share any of your feelings. This place is for people to connect, to understand each other's feelings. This is a friendly zone. The main reason this place is here is for people who need a small push away from a tragedy, or an impending problem. This isn't a loony bin; it's a place to get help. With that, we're going to have everybody introduce themselves, saying their names, then giving a short bio about who they are.

"Jerry Spidelman... I guess I like to... read?"

"Marissa Bates. I like to party, and get crazy! (No pun intended)."

"Teagan. Teagan Hunter. I really like to watch T.V."

"Adrian Bratschi. I like Pentatonix, and other bands. I like to write fan fictions as well, and used to like to read, well... ask my old friend Aria about that."

That was all of the people in the group. There weren't as many as Isaac thought, and he wondered how many people total were in the asylum. However, he didn't ask this question. If he even opened his mouth, Matt would be the one who was really speaking. It would be out of his body, with his voice, but it wasn't him. It was another body, but a spiritual one. "So, Isaac, tell us about yourself." His thoughts were cut off, and he looked up to see that everybody was gazing at him. He kept his mouth shut, and the therapist asked again. He wasn't sure what to do, so he just shrugged, looking down at his feet. His therapist asked a third time, but then she said that some people were shy, so they left him be.

Isaac had barely escaped that one. He had to figure out what to do with Matt soon, otherwise he would get in huge trouble. To distract himself, he thought about whether the therapist was a man or a woman. Finally, after much consideration in almost no time, he decided that she was a female. Once again, he was cut off mid-thought. "So, Isaac, do you know why you're in here?" Isaac shrugged once again, and the therapist looked at him intently. "Say something, Isaac. Anything." Before he could think, his mouth automatically opened, and he let it slip.

"You're a b****."

The therapist looked offended for a second, and her face turned sour, but after another minute she calmed down. She looked at him with an eerily calm expression. "See, Isaac? This support group is to help you let go of your true feelings. Now that you've said that about me, what can we do to help change your opinion?"

"Matt is in this room right now! He's a terrifying pyramid figure, but he isn't a prism. He doesn't separate color; he is color himself. He is the true God, the Satan of the over world. He'll get me, I just know it! Help me! HELP ME! HELP ME

RIGHT NOW! By the way, are you a man or a woman?"

The therapist looked at Isaac like he was from another planet, and then she stood up, pulling him to another room. This one looked like a regular doctor's office, and he knew that something bad was going to happen. A few minutes later, he was greeted by a man dressed in a white lab coat, and he was told to lie down, which he did. He was examined for a minute, and then he was asked to speak. He tried not to say anything, but once again Matt prevailed. "Matt, the pyramid, is here right now! Monsters, bees! He took the cake and stuffed it in the gorilla in the corner's mouth."

The doctor exchanged glances with his assistant who had just walked in the room, and they went to the corner and conversed for a bit. During this time, Isaac thought about Matt's strength. It was getting stronger, and he couldn't do anything about it. He now couldn't physically control his mouth, and he wondered what would happen next. Would he be forced to physically harm someone? Would he be forced to kill his own parents by Matt, the sickest figure in all of existence? Would he have to do that?

As if he was on cue, Isaac involuntarily stood up, looking at the two doctors that were quietly talking. He crept towards them, even though he didn't want to, and his fist flew at one of them, connecting with his jaw. He stepped back, finally controlling his body for a second, and he was immediately seized. He was clawing and screaming, two things that Matt were doing to him as well, and he was knocked out via injection from the doctor's assistant.

A white room, covered in padding.

This was where Isaac woke up. He looked around to see that he was completely closed in, except for a door that was ten feet in front of him. He tried to stand up and walk towards it, but he instantly realized that he was in a straitjacket. He had a feeling that he was being watched, and he looked into the top right corner of the room, relative to where he was, and he saw a camera. It was pointed directly at him, so he tried as hard as he could to act natural. Or, at least, natural for a regular person who woke up in a straitjacket. He changed his mind at this and slowly went towards the door, and after a few minutes, he was at his destination. He did his best to hit at the handle, but with the bondage on, it was impossible. He gave up and slumped down, feeling despondent and hopeless.

Isaac sat for a half an hour, thinking about how he had gotten to this point. He had started dreaming, and then he met Andre. He made a few mistakes along the way, like talking to Derek, but otherwise there was nothing that he could do. Matt had taken over his body, and now he was in an insane asylum. He looked up at the camera again, desperate for a way out of his situation. Suddenly, the door creaked open, cutting off all of his thoughts.

Andre.

He stood gloriously in the doorway, the fluorescent lights above him shining brilliantly down on his body, displaying heroism and courage. He stood like this for a second, and then he ran over to Isaac, punching him in the face. Isaac fell to the ground and shrieked at the searing pain coursing through his body. He looked back at Andre, and he opened his mouth to say something.

"Andre! You have to get me out of here. Matt Strange is-"

"I know. I bought you some time. Now, we have to go!"

Isaac was grabbed by Andre and practically dragged out of the room. He was pulled down a large hallway, but he was tackled by two security guards. Andre tased them and continued dragging him through the hallway. He stopped momentarily to put on a mask, and then he continued on, not looking behind him. Isaac tried to look behind Andre for support, but that was impossible with his straitjacket still on.

Matt kicked back in, and Isaac thrashed and struggled against his friend's grasp. He let out a loud shout, and he punched him in the nose, running back the other direction. However, he couldn't run very fast with his bondage on, and Andre caught up with him. He was slammed in the face multiple times, and he couldn't handle it. After another minute of struggle, he became dizzy, and everything fell black.

Isaac woke up in a room he didn't recognize. He was lying on a twin size mattress, underneath a "Star Wars" blanket. He looked around, scanning his surroundings. To his right was Andre, sitting in a chair, a dresser behind him. To his left was a plain white wall, and-

Wait.

He turned back to face Andre. ANDRE. He had been in a daze yesterday, and he barely remembered anything. He looked at him, and immediately asked him why he was here. He didn't know what to ask, and he just wanted to hear his voice again. Andre replied back. "I'll tell you about it later. For now, you need to get some rest. How do you feel?" He started to remember more and more of the previous events, and he realized that he was able to speak again. "Why isn't Matt interfering with my speech?" "I figured out something. I'll tell you all about it later, but you need to rest now..."

"Okay."

"Good. Now be quiet. My parents don't know that you're here."

Isaac turned towards the wall and tried to go to sleep, even though he knew that it wouldn't be possible. Instead, his mind wandered through what had happened lately. Matt had told him that Andre was dead. Was that a lie, or had he came back from the dead? He thought about Matt, and he remembered the other pyramid that was also in the school, that fateful day. He wondered what had happened to that figure, but he quickly dismissed the thought before his mind could wander to other things. He thought some more about Andre, wondering how he had gotten to the asylum. He hadn't of just rode a bike, right? These questions bogged his mind down as he slowly dozed off, remembering that the next day was a Saturday.

Isaac was trapped in darkness, but he wasn't tied up in any way. He could move around, and he could visibly see that he was in an endless void. He explored for a bit, but he was completely alone. He turned around, and Andre appeared in front of him. They were now the only ones in a pool of nothingness, surrounded by an intense shade of pitch black. They both looked at each other, and Andre was the one to speak first.

"Is this dream lucid for you too?"

"Yeah."

"Has it always been like this?"

"Yup." Isaac was afraid of Andre being in this dream, but he didn't know why. They continued to look around together, searching for something that could tell them where they were. They even tried doing what they had done in that other infinite void, but it didn't work. They were powerless, aimless, and had no idea where they were. All they could do was walk around, observing the surroundings around them. The darkness was almost comforting to Isaac. It was the one calm and controlled thing he had in a world of recent terrors and nightmares, slowly withering him away on the inside. He knew that he would either have more chaos or die, though, so he continued to search around even more. He turned towards

Andre, observing his slow motion, the calmness in his search, and he wondered what he was thinking. He stopped for a moment, and Andre stopped as well.

"What's up?"

"Andre, you never told me what you did to stay alive against Matt."

"I told you, it's a long story."

"Tell me anyway."

Andre hesitated for a second, but then he began to speak. "I'm going to start from the very beginning of that day. Once upon a time, Andre Gonzalez was riding his bike to school, ready to begin another day..."

Chapter Twenty-One

An Explanation

Andre looked at Isaac intently. He was hesitant of telling his story, but he had to. He had to make Isaac fully trust him. He had refused to speak at first, but now was a good time. He couldn't run any further.

Isaac listened as Andre spoke, doing his best to show that he was interested. He was, of course, but he was also exhausted, and he didn't feel like listening to a story. Still, he had to. He needed to know what had happened between Andre and Matt, and more importantly, he had to figure out where Matt was. Another minute went by, and it was at that point that Andre begun. "I'm going to start from the very beginning of that day. Once upon a time, I was riding my bike to school, ready to start my day. After a few minutes, I finally got to school, and I walked inside the building. I was a bit late, as my alarm hadn't gone off, so I rushed off to class."

"He was upon me in an instant. I looked up to see that Matt was on top of me, and I flew a punch to his face. He flied back, but he grabbed my arms, forcing me to become vulnerable. He hit me in the stomach, and I doubled over in pain. It was at that moment that he slammed his fist on my head, and everything went black."

"I woke up, looking around me. I had no idea where I was. To my right was pitch black, and that was also to my left. I looked out in front of me, now not in a complete daze, and there Matt stood, gazing me directly in the eye. I could see fire in his pupils, blazing powerfully, causing an intense glow. He was determined to get his way, so whenever he spoke, I listened to what he had to say. 'Listen here, buddy. For about a month now I've been chasing both you and Isaac. You may be wondering; if I have magical powers, why haven't I just killed you yet? Well, I'm gonna spill the beans. I need at least one of you to take over this world. With two of you it's easier, but I can do it in one pretty easily as well. I'm telling you this now because I wanted to play with you, but now I've calmed down. I'm not playing games anymore.'"

"Matt continued to speak to me, but his tone became even more intense, his stern expression piercing through my eyes, my soul.'I'm gonna cut you a deal. I'll leave one of you alive and one dead, and I've chosen you to be alive. All I need you to do is mess with Isaac, and then kill him. I have him kidnapped right now! Now, you may be wondering, why haven't I killed him yet? And, speaking truthfully here, I have tried to kill him before. The reason that I can't kill Isaac is because there's something inside him, some kind of power that I don't have. I can't kill him. But if you do, and you help me take over this godforsaken planet, then I'll not only let you stay alive, but you can have anything you want in the world. Anything!' Matt smiled, holding out his hand, which glowed brilliantly in the darkness of where I was. 'So, what'ya say, Andre?' I looked at him, unsure of what to do, but I knew that he couldn't be trusted. 'No!' I yelled. 'I would never partner up with you!' His expression immediately turned from happiness to anger and lust, and he glared at me, visible frustrated. His hand turned into a ball of fire, and he pointed it directly at me. 'I COULD KILL YOU IN AN INSTANT! YOU NEED TO LISTEN TO ME; I AM YOUR SUPERIOR!'"

"I stopped for a second, closing my eyes, cringing, waiting for him to kill me. But then I realized something: he needed me. Without me, he would never convince you to side with him, because he couldn't kill him. He would have to get someone else to kill him, to do his bidding, but it wasn't going to be me. No matter what I said or did, I wouldn't have killed you. I decided to act like I didn't have this knowledge, and I looked directly at Matt, finally saying the decisive eight words that would change its whole reality. 'Okay. Give me a knife, and I'll kill Isaac.'"

"Matt held out his hand for me to shake, and after a second our hands connected. As soon as I shook it, I felt a strange energy, almost like I was being controlled, and then the whole void turned into a gray room. It was empty, except for a tennis ball in the corner and you, blindfolded and in shackles. Matt leaned close to me, whispering in my ear. 'There's no rush... Don't be doing anything funny, cause' I'll be watching you...' Matt went out the door, and I looked at you again. I wanted to survive, but I didn't trust Matt, and would killing you be worth it? Would taking one life be worth living my own? What made me different? I picked up the tennis ball in the corner and bounced it against the back wall. I was going to show Matt that I wanted to kill you, but I wasn't really going to. I was going to trick him. I held the knife close to you, its shiny blade slightly connecting with your skin. I looked at you again, but I instantly turned my head behind me, looking for it, who wasn't there. I stepped back, and I taunted you, talking about how you were going to die. Then I spoke quickly, telling you about the dangers that were coming your way. Before I could save you, Matt came in, forcing me out of the room."

"I was dragged out of the room, forced out into a large hallway, with many doors that were open. As I was pulled through, I saw that each of them contained my memories, my thoughts, until the very last door. Behind it was Matt dragging me down the hallway, and I gasped. It had all of my memories, my thoughts, my dreams and desires, all stored in its own sick domain. It knew what I was going to do the whole time, and it had waited for me to prove it. I tried thinking of the clock again, or anything to help me in my situation, but help was nonexistent; it wasn't the void world, and I couldn't imagine anything anymore. Finally, the hallway ended, and I was pulled through the very last door, which was perpendicular to all of the other ones. I was dragged into a small room, containing a seat, and I was strapped in forcibly by Matt."

"I was terrified, and I wondered if I should've trusted Matt. I feel bad for it, I'm sorry, but I generally considered the thought that killing you was the right thing to do. I looked directly at it as it entered my mouth, and I swallowed. I had no idea what was happening, and now I was only looking at a concrete wall. I tried to cry for help, but all that came out of my mouth was what it was saying. 'Testing, testing, one two three... Eureka! This works!' I immediately shut my mouth, but it was forced open again, and I was unable to control my words. It was at that moment that I had an epiphany. Every single moment of my life was a game. It was an enormous chess match, and Matt was a grand master. I couldn't read its thoughts, but I could predict them. It was not to be trusted, and just as I realized this I punched myself in the face. I had to do whatever I could to get it out! Slowly, my hand started to glow the same red hue as Matt had glowed earlier, and I was unable to control it. I took my other hand and pried it open, and then I forced it to punch myself in the face."

"I slumped over, exhausted, and glanced over at my hand. It was still glowing, and I tried to speak. 'Hello?' That was what I had meant to say, and I quickly realized that I had beaten Matt out of my body. I looked over at my seat, and realized that I had broken from the ropes that bound my wrists to the seat. Then, I saw that I had just slipped out of them, as they were extremely loose. I slipped my wrists in and out, and I chuckled. It felt forced, but I needed to laugh, badly."

"It was at that moment that a different pyramid figure came out. It looked like Matt, but with a more friendly expression. Before I could say or do anything, it began to speak to me in distress. 'I know you don't trust me, but I sense the end is near. I know Isaac, and I know Matt. Matt can't be trusted. You need to listen to me.'"

"I couldn't say or do anything in protest before I was dragged out of the room. I went through one of the doors, and the regular world appeared around me. I was completely alone, and I was sneaked into my house by the figure. 'By the way, Andre, my name's Holt. Holt Egnarts.' I watched as the figure disappeared, telling me to keep my place and identity a secret."

"That was exactly what I did. I didn't know this figure, but it had told me not to trust Matt, which I already knew, so maybe I could trust it. For the next few days, I hid myself on the streets. I heard you calling for me once, and I desperately hid behind a tree, wanting to meet up with you again. My heart longed for someone that I knew and could trust, but I had a strangely good feeling about Holt."

"After a few more days, maybe a week or so, I don't remember, Holt came back. I was digging through a dumpster whenever he appeared around me, and he grabbed my hand. The world turned into a mental institution, and I was unsure what to do. I looked at Holt, and it began to talk to me. 'Andre. Look at me. You have to listen to every single word that I say, okay?' I nodded. 'Good. Now, listen to me. Matt is inside Isaac, just like he was with you. Isaac couldn't fight him off, and it forced him to be put here. He's in solitary confinement. Room 1-112. If you can convince them to let you visit, then you can punch him in the face. The power that you've gotten from Matt is weakened, but it'll work for a little while longer. You have to get him out of here. Now go! You don't have much time.'"

"I sprinted to room 1-112, and I convinced the people to let me visit. They didn't want me in, but I began to cry, as I badly needed to cry, and they exchanged glances. Finally, the unlocked the door, giving me five minutes. I walked into the room, and I immediately grabbed you, punching you in the face. I had to get you out of this area. I grabbed you, pulling you out of the room, and the power that Matt had inadvertently given me gave me the strength to fight off the security guards. I realized that my hand was like a taser for the time being, so I was careful. You began to fight me, and I punched you again. I eventually got you out of the building, where Holt was waiting for us."

"Holt took us both, and we appeared in my room. I told me to keep him a secret, and then he left. I looked at you again, and you woke up, in a daze. I told you to keep quiet, and that I would explain the story later."

"Now here we are."

Chapter Twenty-Two

Unsure

Isaac sat up, gazing at a wall that was unfamiliar to him. He glanced over to his right, searching for a clock, but he didn't find it. He realized that he was lying on the ground, a blanket both underneath of him and on top of him. He looked to his left to see Andre, lying in his bed, and he recapped what had happened in his dream.

I was trapped in an infinite void. I searched around for a while, but I couldn't find anything that wasn't just darkness and empty space. After a while, Andre appeared, for reasons that weren't explained, and we looked around together. I asked him how he had managed to survive, and he told me the whole story, starting from whenever Matt had taken him hostage. Then, after the story, I woke up.

Isaac tapped on Andre's shoulder, waking him up, and he quickly hid whenever his friend's parents walked in. He waited as they told him to wake up, and he realized that they had brought him breakfast in bed. They must have thought that he deserved it, because he had been missing for a while. Being missing can be a traumatic experience, and some people need comfort after it. However, Andre was okay, but his parents were still being careful. "Andre... How are you feeling?"

"Good," Andre replied. He didn't know what else to say, because in reality he felt weird. He remembered the dream as well.

"You know we love you, right?" His parents asked.

"Of course!"

His parents exchanged momentary glances, and then they looked back at him. "So," his mother asked, "The police need to know; what happened whenever you got kidnapped?"

Andre was unsure of what to do. Isaac sat and watched as he fabricated an answer, doing something to get both the police and his parents off of his back. "Well... It's hard to talk about, but... a man in that same 2005 Honda Accord took me hostage."

"What did he look like?"

211

"Well... I didn't know, because he was wearing a black mask, and dark glasses. His body was covered in black robes."

"Good," his father replied to his answer. "We'll make sure to contact the police about the incident. In the meantime, enjoy your breakfast. You probably need to rest... Oh, and by the way, we're gonna be gone for a bit; we have to go grocery shopping."

"I sure do need the rest..."

"Love you."

"Love you too."

With that, Andre's parents walked out of the room, and he looked at Isaac. Isaac was still hiding behind the dresser, and after a few seconds he stood up, stretching his legs.

The day went by as normally as it could. It was a sweltering Saturday, and Isaac was doing his best to hide from people. He and Andre discussed the dream, but they were unsure of what to do, so they just decided to wait.

The next morning, Isaac and Andre were talking again. Isaac stated to keep watch of anything suspicious, and Andre agreed. They had to be careful. They had to stay alive.

Before any of them could say another word, he was knocked to the ground by a mini swirling storm, and he looked up to see Holt in his wake, struggling to keep its composure. It looked at both Isaac and Andre, and without protest it grabbed them both.

"You have to come now. Matt is back, and he's weaker, but-"

All three of them were knocked down, and now Matt came into the room. It looked at the three people on the floor, strewn about like crumbs dropped from a piece of bread. It released a wicked grin, placing its hands together. It rubbed them, causing the intense friction of how fast it rubbed them creating a ball of fire, and it shot it straight at Holt.

Before Holt could react, the ball of fire slammed it square in the face, and it fell over, trying not to release a scream in pure agony. Time seemed to stand still for a moment, and all four of them heard Andre's parents pull their car out of the driveway, leaving temporarily. Holt let out a deafening screech, and Matt slammed into it, the fight between the two figures beginning.

Holt and Matt were all over each other, clawing and screaming, and they were using magic as well. Andre and Isaac tried to help Holt, but they were quickly pushed back. All they could do was watch in horror as Holt was devoured by

Matt, and the last thing it could do before it died, its last burst of pure energy, was to send Isaac to a safe haven, a void, and after another second Andre was there as well.

"What took you so long?" Isaac asked.

"It only took me a second to get here," Andre replied. "I guess time passes slower in here..."

They looked around for what felt like forever, but in reality was only a few seconds, trying to find a way out of their void. They knew that Holt had sent them here to be safe, but they were stuck. Even trying to imagine something to help them wouldn't work, as they couldn't do that. They were in a truly infinite void, and without the help of Holt, the only other magical being that they knew. Without its help, they were stuck for the rest of their lives.

Isaac turned his head to the right, looking at Andre. He thought about the dream that they must have shared, and he asked him the decisive question. "Andre, you never told me how you got here."

Andre looked over at Isaac. "Didn't I already tell you?" Isaac was unsure what to say, but he didn't remember the exact details. "I don't remember exactly," he said.

Andre heaved a long and heavy sigh, and he told Isaac about what had happened for the second time. He had been taken by Matt, forced to view Isaac being held up in shackles, and he was offered to kill him. He played dumb, but Matt found figured out his head somehow, and he was taken to another room, where his mouth was entered, and he could be controlled. Then, Holt helped him escape, and he was taken to the insane asylum, where he had to grab Isaac, then sprinting out of the building, being taken to his house.

Isaac thought about this story for a second, and he realized how Andre got the power. "You shook his hand," he stated. "Something must have entered you, giving him the ability to read your mind, and you the ability to get him out." Andre discovered that Isaac was right, and he looked to his left at him, momentarily thinking, then responding to the statement. "You're right... Do you think he can read my mind still?"

"I doubt it. If you lost your ability to stop him, then he probably lost the ability to read your mind. Besides, if he could, wouldn't he have used that to his advantage?"

"You're right."

After that short discussion, both Isaac and Andre became silent. There was really nothing to talk about, as they both were thinking the same thing, a feeling of fear and anxiety, so the only communication they had was occasionally glancing over at each other. They wanted to stay together, a unit. They couldn't be separated again.

"ISAAC! ANDRE!"

Both of them slowly turned their heads, recognizing the familiar voice they had just heard.

Matt.

Both Isaac and Andre turned back around, and they ran for their lives. Matt had magical powers, and if they got to close, then they risked getting killed in some horrible way. They sprinted until they couldn't breathe anymore, and they looked back to see that Matt was right on top of them. However, instead of killing them, it stopped. It appeared to be in deep thought, and Isaac shuddered, wondering what it was thinking. Both of the teenagers were frozen in fear, and the fact that they were now being offered a deal didn't help.

"Listen here, Isaac and Andre," Matt said, the same calm tone as it did with Andre earlier. "I didn't want to come to this, but I'm gonna give you guys the deal of a lifetime. *Literally*." Matt furrowed its eyebrows whenever he said 'literally,' because it wanted to create emphasis. It stared at both

Isaac and Andre for a minute, and then it continued. "I've always been able to take over the world. My magic powers allow me to do so, right? Well, it's hard to do that with just myself. You see, I can't get to the normal world without you two. You both act as keys, as ways for me to cross over. However, in order to do that, you'd have to let me." Matt held out its hand, and Isaac and Andre both took a step back. "Shake my hand, as a sign of good will, and then we'll continue." They shook their heads, glancing over at each other. They weren't about to accidentally let Matt into their minds. They had to remain strong.

Matt looked at both of them, its smile turning into a frown. "I could kill you in an instant. I'll give you two choices: You could let me through, let me take over the world, and rule it with me. I will let you reign as kings, living in the finest of conditions. Or, on the other hand, you can not let me have access, and," it held up his hand again, electric sparks coming out of it, "Let's just say... Bad things will happen to both you and your family."

"How can we trust you?" Andre asked, looking flustered. Matt replied back solemnly. "Because," it hesitated, "I can still take over the world, and if I wanted to kill you only, then why didn't I already?"

Isaac sat, unsure of what to do. On one hand, Matt seemed to be telling the truth, but on the other, it was obvious that it was lying. Could it really take over the world without them? If it was hard, then wouldn't it really be able to take the risk? He thought for another moment, and then he came to the conclusion that it was lying. It had to be!

Right?

Andre held out his hand. Isaac saw this, and he immediately lunged forward, trying to stop the deal from happening. Both Andre and Matt were knocked to the ground, and Andre was the first to realize what was happening. He shot up, tackling it to the ground. He drove his fist into its body, and he accidentally hit a button labeled *Communications.* A series of names popped up. They were people that Matt had communicated with.

Donna Crowley.
David Crowley.
Pedro Gonzalez.
Clara Gonzalez.
Andre Gonzalez.
Derek Howard.
Max Barton.
Isaac Crowley.

Andre tried to hide Matt's body from Isaac's view. He couldn't have Isaac figure out his secret, as that would destroy everything that he was doing. Weeks ago, he was promised to be a part of the new world, and he couldn't have that stopped now. He had to hide the module, and he tried to close it, but Matt was frozen in place, in time. Isaac walked over, wailing on it.

Isaac punched and kicked Matt's body as hard as he could. This was his chance to defeat it, to finally stop the dreams. He saw Andre on top of it as well, but he was covering something.

"What's underneath your stomach?"

"Nothing, just the same old body..."

Isaac walked over, and he tried to push Andre aside, but he was tackled, being pinned to the ground. He looked over at him, who was trying to knock him out, but he dodged the punch, lunging over to the module just in time. He read the names in his head as quickly as he could, and he dodged another punch as he looked at Andre in disbelief. It was all a lie, everything that he knew. Andre was a fake.

A feeling of dread and mistrust was the last thing that Isaac felt as he was slammed on the head. The last thing he heard before everything went black was Andre's menacing laugh, and he knew that there was no one he could really trust. He let out a cry for help, but he quickly slumped on the ground, blood rushing out of his head, breathing what he thought would be his last breath.

Chapter Twenty-Three

An Epiphany

Isaac tried to sit up, but his head slammed on metal and he fell over. He rubbed the spot where it had connected with his head, and he lied down. There was barely enough room for him to stretch out his legs, and he looked around. He was stuck inside a metal cage, and he reached his free hand out, feeling for the lock. He found it, and he quietly wished that he had the key. He scanned his surroundings outside the cage, and he saw multiple tables and chairs laid out in a small room, but he couldn't see the edges of it. It was surrounded by wall of fire, and there was no space for a door anywhere. He wondered if he was set here to die.

Before he could think anymore, a small tornado appeared by one of the tables, and Matt came into the room. It looked around, finally resting its eyes directly on him, squinting. It leaned down, and Andre appeared at another table, then Isaac's parents at another, and afterwards, Andre's parents appeared as well. The last person to appear was Derek, and Isaac narrowed his eyes at all of them, giving them the middle finger. They had betrayed his trust, and his parents had even tried to put him in a mental institution, and now he hated them all. He had to say something to them, to get his frustrations out. "Why? Why did you do it?"

Andre was the first to reply, a cocky grin spreading off of the face that Isaac now wanted to punch. "Whenever Matt takes over the new world, we'll be the kings and queens. We'll be the ones who survive, who drive the remaining slaves to do our bidding. We'll survive the inevitable fire of this world, and there's nothing that you can do about it."

"But still," Isaac yelled, "How can there be an end of the world, if I'm the access for it?! Didn't you bother to think any of this through?" Matt looked at him, and it released a wicked laugh, ringing through his ears. "I guess you don't get it, Isaac... I can force you to let me through you, and there's nothing that you can do about it. Let's just get this over with. Shake my hand."

"Never!"

"But Isaac," his mother stated, "he can force you to do it anyways. We just want you to have it a bit easier."

"If you can take over the world without me, then just do it! I won't help you and your evil plans!"

Matt glanced over at all of the people sitting by the tables, and he looked back at Isaac. "I'm gonna cut you a deal," he said. "I'll still take over the world without you, but it's easier for me to get to the world with your help. If you're a good sport, then, well... I'll let you reign over all of these people. You'll be able to live like a king, hell, you'll be a king! All you have to do is shake my hand..."

Isaac was once again unsure what to do. If Matt could take over the world without him, then why would it want his help? It couldn't be trusted, but he wanted to survive. Could he really become a king? Would it be worth it to have the world end? He gazed at the other people in the room, and he had an epiphany.

"He's lying to you, all of you! Why would you trust him, after everything that's happened? How could you trust him?"

It was Derek's turn to speak. "Isaac, I'm gonna have to come clean. We knew from the beginning about what was happening. We knew that you were going to have the dreams. We knew that Lucy would die. In fact, Max was the driver in that car! Max killed Lucy!"

Isaac's head was spinning wildly. He thought about all of the things that had happened, all of the dreams. He thought about Lucy's death, the black 2005 Honda Accord, how the police could never quite catch it. He thought about Andre, how he had trusted him, and then his mind switched to Derek. He knew about the dreams before he had told him! Everything that he knew was a lie, and there was no one he could trust. Everyone that he had known had betrayed him, all for greed. They were blind, and they didn't see the bigger picture. They didn't know anything about what Matt would do to them.

"Isaac," Andre cut him off, in the middle of thought, "remember whenever I told you to trust your gut? Well, Matt, would you like to finish?"

"Sure!" Matt replied, its piercing gaze shooting straight through Isaac's eyes, directly into his soul, "I put those gut feelings into you. I am the reason for the dreams, for all of the feelings that you had. It was all a part of a big game, and I wanted to wait to spill the beans myself, but since you saw who you can't trust, well, you're welcome!"

Isaac once again looked at everybody. "How can you trust him? Don't you know he's lying to you? Can't you figure out that you're all a part of his sick game? He will dump all of you as soon as he gets the chance!"

"That's a good point," Andre's father replied, "But what's better: knowing that you're gonna be a part of the people who die, or taking a risk to survive, to live like a king for the rest of your long and prosperous life?"

Isaac had to think about this. Andre's father almost had a good point, but it wasn't good enough. "Yeah, but without you, he wouldn't be able to get to me! He would be stuck in the passage between Earth, and, wherever he exists! But now, because of you guys, he was able to get to here!"

Andre looked down, but he was still smiling. "Actually, Isaac, it was me. I was the one who gave Matt access..."

"How?!"

"Well, it's simple, really. You know how you think I have knowledge on an astronomical level, well, I don't just have that. I'm not, really, from here..."

"You're from another planet?!"

"Not exactly. I come from the same place that Matt comes from, except, I'm different than it. It's always been known that there's something different about me, something that allows me to come here. So, I am the real link. I am the reason for all of this, for all of your dreams. I was the reason Matt came here."

Isaac was dumbfounded. For all of this time, he thought that Andre was to be trusted, and he certainly thought that he was a human. Now, he wasn't trustworthy, but he also wasn't from Earth! "Andre, how could you?" Isaac asked. "How could you possibly do this to Earth?"

"Power, Isaac. That's my only reason for all of this. I can actually have power, avoid being mistreated by aliens, or humans, or anything. People will bow down before me, not some stupid poser! I'll be the one that people look up to in awe... in jealousy. That's the real reason for all of this, even with Matt, with anybody here! They want power, the one thing that all humans want. Some, like us, will do anything for it."

"That's sick! Power isn't a justifiable reason to do this to anybody! I thought... I thought that you were my friend. Mom, dad, I thought that... that... that I could trust you..."

Isaac broke out into tears. Out of everything that had happened to him in the past month, with Lucy dying, him having these dreams, being attacked by Max, and almost being ran over multiple times, he badly needed to express some kind of emotion. He wished for somebody, anybody, to comfort him. He needed someone to come by his side, to be his aid, someone that he could trust. But, he didn't have that; there was nobody. Even though there were other people in the world, he didn't know any of them, and they'd all think that he was crazy. They wouldn't see him as a person, but instead as an animal, someone crazy who needed to be locked up. He was truly alone.

"Mom, dad," Isaac asked, wiping away the tears, "after all of our memories, you're really willing to do this? You're really willing to aid to the end of the world, the end of me?

"Yes," his mother replied, "I'm willing to do this. We all are..."

"You can still stop this! It's not too late!" Isaac knew that he was at a major disadvantage, but he had to find some way to convince at least one person that Matt wasn't to be trusted. How could they be so ignorant, so... naive?

Isaac once again looked at everybody in the crowd, but his eyes eventually rested on Derek. His oldest friend that he used to have. He looked at him sadly, wishing for him to come back. He needed someone on his side. Before he could say anything anymore, Derek frowned, looking at Matt. He looked back at Isaac, and a feeling of regret flushed over him. He turned his head towards Matt again, and he stood up, climbing out of his seat, walking towards it.

It all happened too fast. Isaac could only watch as Derek walked over to Matt. He tackled it, pushing it over, and he wailed on it, punching, kicking, clawing and screaming. He even bit it. It quickly shot up, holding lightning in its hand, and it flashed him, burning him to pieces.

"WELL," it asked, "DOES ANYONE ELSE WANT A PIECE OF ME?! I CAN DUMP ALL OF YOU RIGHT NOW IF I WANT!" A wicked grin spread across its face, and it scanned everybody again. "I just realized it... I don't need any of you anymore. You've all provided the links that I need..."

Matt raised its hand, shooting a ball of fire out of it, directly towards Andre, but he dove to the side just as he could. It began to shoot multiple balls of fire and lightning, but it was tackled from behind, and It fell to the ground. It looked at Isaac again, and the last thing he could sense was the feeling of being shocked, and then he closed his eyes, coming into a bright light.

Isaac had no idea where he was. He looked to his left, to his right, and even behind him, but he was trapped in the void again. He sat down, and he thought about what had happened. Could he really trust his friends and family again, or was it all just more simulation? After spilling the beans, would they continue to make him think that he could trust them?

Isaac walked around some more, and he even tried imagining a clock, but it didn't come. He waited for something to happen, but it didn't. He was stuck again, until Matt brought him out. For now, he sat still, thinking about what had happened. He had been betrayed by all the people that he trusted, and he was played for a fool. He cursed himself for being so ignorant, but he knew that it wasn't his fault. What was he expected to do? He didn't know about anything that was in the theoretical cosmos besides what he learned in school, and he was now being forced to learn so much in so little time.

Isaac lay down on the ground, wishing for someone to come in and save him. It was one thing to be fighting, but another to be stuck in an infinite void, left to rot. For now, he closed his eyes, giving his brain a break. He had to sleep. He had to figure out what was happening, and how he could logically stop it. There was a way; he just had to find it.

C h a p t e r   T w e n t y - F o u r

Consequences

Isaac was trapped in the same infinite void that he always knew, the same place that he had no idea where he was. He didn't have anyone around him, and he was surrounded by darkness as far as the eye could see. He had looked around earlier, but it was always the same. There was nothing to find. The world was a barren landscape, and he was completely alone.

Before he could think anymore, the universe swirled around him, and he felt incredibly sick. First there was fire, and then the room appeared. He was out of the cage, sitting in one of the desks, and he looked out in front of him, seeing his parents, Andre, and Andre's parents, all wailing at Matt. Derek was dead in the corner, blood leaking out of his battered skull. Isaac continued to sit still, and he was unsure of whether or not to enter the fight. They looked like they needed his help, but he was afraid to get hurt. Besides, if his hand was touched by Matt, then it would have the key into getting into the normal world. It would be able to take over the world without anybody's help.

Isaac had to take the risk. His parents and friends needed his help, and, even though they betrayed him, he sensed that they had found the error in their ways. He slowly walked up to the battle, careful to keep both of his hands in his pockets. Then, he wondered something. Why hadn't it gotten access whenever it shook Andre's hand? He realized that the power was only temporary, and it had forgotten to act at that moment. He walked towards Matt, and he slammed it directly in the face, causing it to double back. He kicked it, and its eyes locked into his, and he took a step backwards. It was upon him now, but Andre and his parents quickly threw it off.

Isaac and Matt both gazed at each other intently, still in their own tension. The rest of the people then continued to fight, knocking it down to the ground. It looked at Isaac, who followed suit in the beating, punching it directly in the eye. He punched it again, and it let out a shriek in pain, releasing a fireball, directly at Andre.

Andre was blasted to the adjacent wall, but Isaac didn't have time to worry about that. He continued to look at Matt, and he accidentally touched another one of its modules, labeled *Destruction.* He grabbed its arm, careful not to touch its hand, and he touched the button labeled *Fireball.* A ball of fire flew directly at its eye, and it connected.

It all happened before Isaac could even think. Matt began to burn up, first the eye, and then continuing on to its abdomen, causing the modules to short out. Before it could die, Isaac pressed a button labeled *Isaac's room*, and his own room appeared, on planet Earth. It still burned up, the rest of the modules shorting out, and the fire spread to the base of its body, where it let out a final scream in pure terror and pain.

And then it was dead.

Isaac watched calmly as it said its final words, managing to let one last thing out. "YOU DON'T UNDERSTAND, DO YOU?! THERE ARE MORE- YOU WILL... DIE..." That was the last thing it said before it burned up the rest of the way, and Isaac's parents grabbed a fire extinguisher, stopping the flames before they could spread any further.

Isaac looked at the rest of the group, and they looked back, solemn expressions on their faces. His parents wrapped their arms around him, and so did Andre's parents. However, there was no cheer. There were only soft tears of both sadness and relief, and it took a couple minutes before anybody thought of Andre.

Isaac sprinted up to him, tears gushing down his face. He was thankful to see he was still alive, but he was hurt badly. He had burn wounds all over his body, and he was barely breathing. Isaac pulled his phone out of his pocket, and he dialed 911, calling for some kind of medical attention, anything. He had to help Andre. He had to keep him alive, even if it took a while to recover. He couldn't lose what was now his only true friend.

Andre tilted his neck toward Isaac, trying his best to keep his burn pain to a minimum. However, that was near impossible with how bad it was, so he let out a small shriek in pain, then backing back down again, speaking. "Isaac... I'm sorry. I'm so sorry. I shouldn't have done that, betrayed you. I got greedy, wanting power and respect. I deserve to-to... die..."

"Andre! No, I have an ambulance coming for you. You'll be fine, but you're gonna have to hang in there. Can you do that for me, please?"

Andre sighed, resting his hand on the floor but immediately regretting it. Pain shot up his arm, and he brought it back up, looking at Isaac again. "Isaac, I'm sorry... Just listen to me. I did this to you; I brought on these dreams, all for my own selfish purposes. It's all my fault and I deserve to die. Please... just let me pay for what I've done..."

Isaac decided to let the ambulance come anyway. Andre had to survive. After about ten minutes of silence, it did come, and he was sent away, Isaac and his family, including Andre's parents, forced to be with their own thoughts and actions. Then, he thought of Derek, but he was already dead. He had died first.

Isaac took Derek's body and put it in a garbage bag. He had no idea how to embalm, so he and his family cremated it the best they could. They placed the ashes in a wooden box, then spending the rest of the day to dig a six foot deep hole as a group. Finally, Isaac took the box, dropped it into the hole, and everyone filled it in.

There would be police investigations, allegations, questions. Isaac knew this very well, so he decided to think of a plan to fabricate Derek's death. It wasn't right, but he had to figure out a way to get people off his back. He thought about talking to Derek's parents about it, but they didn't know anything about what had happened. They couldn't help him at all, and even if he got everyone that knew to tell them, he couldn't risk them not believing in the story, which seemed very likely.

Isaac thought about faking being Max, but he was dead, so he didn't know what to do. He then realized that the police would want to know where the body was. He quickly realized that he had to talk to Derek's parents, as there was nothing to do, and he thought about any proof that he might have. He found out that he didn't have any, so he gathered everyone that he could, getting them all to come to Derek's house.

Isaac knocked on the door, and both of Derek's parents opened it, looking at the crowd that was in front of them. They exchanged glances, and then his mother said two words.

"We know."

"What?" Isaac replied.

"Yeah. Derek told us what was going to happen, and we almost believed in him. He's not good at lying, and he appeared serious. I figure that this whole crowd is even more proof of what had happened..."

Derek's father chimed in. "Of course... But where is he?"

This was the hardest part to Isaac. He had to tell Derek's parents that their own son was dead, and it would be almost impossible for them to bear, he knew it. He inhaled a deep breath, and he told them the harrowing news that no parent wants to hear. "Your son... is... dead. Matt killed him."

"WHAT?"

Derek's parents tightly embraced each other, tears rushing down their faces, and all they could do was thank Isaac for telling them. They slammed the door, and later came back out, saying that they would handle the whole case of why Derek would be dead. The police would be on them soon, and it was their job to help their son. It was their duty.

That night, Isaac stared up at his ceiling, thinking about all the stuff that had happened. He knew that he wasn't going to have any more dreams, and this made him slightly content as he thought about this, but he still wondered if Andre was okay. He had no idea what was going to happen to him, and a tear trickled down his face. He wished that none of it had happened, yet he was glad that all of it had. He had learned so much about himself, and he had even learned about the higher cosmos. Still, he couldn't tell anyone besides the people that he could trust about what had happened.

The next day, Isaac stayed home from school, and his parents used their sick days to stay home from work. It was a Monday, and even though he would miss an important test, he could make it up. *Stupid language arts teacher,* he thought as he looked out the window.

Later on, while he was eating lunch, the home phone rang, and he shot up from his macaroni and cheese, rushing over. He didn't have caller I.D, so he picked up the phone without knowing who was on the other end.

"Hello?"

"Yes, is this Donna Crowley?"

"No, it's Isaac. I'll go get her."

Isaac sprinted to his mother, who was watching an infomercial for a blender, and he handed her the phone. He tried not to watch her talking, but for some reason it was mesmerizing seeing her in that state.

"Uh-huh. Yeah... Oh! I'll tell Isaac right away."

Isaac's mom walked over to him, and she told him that Andre was available to see in the hospital. The whole family climbed into the car and drove off, going to a place that they hadn't seen in a long time.

Isaac opened the door to the room that Andre was in, and he slowly walked inside. He was terrified at what lay before him. Andre was lying down in a bed, in a controlled state, but his skin was completely red and black. He was in serious pain, but he did his best not to show it as Isaac walked over, trying not to gaze at his burned up friend.

"Go on, look," Andre said. "The doctors say that I'm going to have to get a large-scale surgery, but... a full-on skin surgery has never been successfully attempted before. In case if I die... I need you to do something for me."

Andre reached into his hospital gown pocket, and he pulled out a good luck charm that Isaac knew very well. It was made of emerald, and it shined in the light brilliantly, radiating out in all directions. He placed it in his hand, and said that he had gotten it from Matt. Isaac clasped his hand, holding it close to his heart and closing his eyes, and he tried not to cry. He couldn't remain strong, and he silently bawled, almost hugging Andre, before at the last second remembering the burns that completely covered his body. They both were crying now, and later on, driving home, he held the charm close to his heart. He knew that Lucy was somewhere looking at him, smiling, and he wished that she could be with him.

Finally, it was time to go to bed, so Isaac said "goodnight" to his parents, pulling the covers over him. He still had the charm in his hand, and he wished that he could never let go of it. He said a silent "thank you" to whatever was above him in the heavens, and then he fell asleep, still thinking about everything that had happened, the charm resting in his closed palm.

Chapter Twenty-Five

An Operation

Isaac woke up from a silent and dreamless sleep, looking around his familiar room. In front of him was his usual clock, reading 7:00 A.M. He sat up, climbing out of his bed, and getting dressed. He wore the same outfit that he had the day before Lucy had gotten run over, a bright red shirt, and some normal, boring blue jeans. He took a deep breath, and the aroma of crepes filled his lungs. He rushed downstairs, excited to once again eat his favorite breakfast food with the family that he once again trusted. He sat down at the dining room table, waiting patiently as his parents laid out the various toppings that they would put on the crepes, and finally, the stars of the show.

He watched as his parents sat down, both giving him hugs before they did, and he grabbed a few of the crepes. He put his toppings on them, and he slowly ate his food. There wasn't a single word uttered in the beginning, but he had to eventually break the silence. "So... The doctors say that Andre's surgery is coming soon." His mother perked up, almost spilling her coffee. "Oh! That reminds me. Isaac, the doctors called me late last night. They said that the surgery was scheduled for next Sunday."

This both made Isaac happy, and sent a cold chill down his spine. He sat still for a moment, but then he spoke again. "Can we go to the hospital on that day?" Instead of more talking, both of his parents gave a silent nod, and with that, everyone continued to eat their breakfast. However, they didn't refrain from speaking because it was an awkward meal; instead, they didn't talk because there was nothing else to say. Everyone was thinking the same thing.

Isaac finished his breakfast, and he realized that he was almost late for school. He had to get going. He went into his room, grabbing his backpack, and he entered the car with his parents. Once again, no one said anything as they drove along. But, this time, his parents were listening to the radio.

Isaac had decided to start going back to school as soon as he could. He felt good on

Monday, but his parents wanted him to be with them, so he was. Later on in the day, he wanted to visit Andre, so they did. With the news of Andre's surgery, he wished that he could time travel, but he knew that he couldn't do that. Instead, he just let it be as he went along to school, pushing the thought out of his mind.

Isaac got out of the car, walking up to the familiar high school building where he spent most of his days. The bell rang, and he walked inside with no one to keep him company. Lucy had been ran over by a car, Max killed, Derek blasted away, and Andre burned into the hospital. And, all of his other friends had betrayed him on speech day, all just because he was friends with Andre. He didn't care about them anymore; they were fools for making fun of him just because his opinions were different than theirs. He scoffed at their thoughts, taking his time to go to his locker. Everyone around him was acting normally, just like nothing had happened. However, he knew about things that no one else besides his parents and some other adults were aware of, and nothing would ever be the same to him again. He wondered if he could ever feel normal again, but he decided that the best thing to do was act normal. If he acted normal, then maybe he would eventually feel like it.

Isaac walked into his language arts classroom, and nobody questioned why Andre was absent. Nobody cared, nobody wanted to figure out what had happened. But, he knew that there would be investigations into the incident. The police would question him, and he would have to be careful. He knew that Andre or his parents wouldn't press charges, though, so it probably wasn't a big deal.

"Good morning, class." The language arts teacher said, cutting Isaac off in thought as people always did. "I hope that you have good knowledge of what we've been learning. Get out a piece of paper."

Isaac pulled out some notebook paper, but his teacher said that he was exempt from the test until he learned what was taught on Monday. This gave him great relief, but he had to spend lunch learning what he had already known. At least their unit was simple.

The whole day seemed to go by incredibly slowly, and Isaac sat with boredom in his last two periods, drawing pictures of Matt. He knew that he was deeply affected by what had happened, and while he didn't need therapy, this would comfort him a little bit. It felt weird to him, but he imagined that the thoughts of Matt inside him were migrating to the paper, leaving his brain in the dust. He wondered if this method of therapy was actually used by psychologists.

Finally, after a couple more hours of pure boredom, the bell for the end of the day finally rang, and Isaac sprinted to his locker. He turned the combination, causing it to open, and he pulled out his backpack. Surprisingly, he didn't have any homework that day, so he didn't have to grab any binders. Instead, he put the jacket that he had used that morning into his pack, and he left the school, climbing into his parents' car.

The rest of the day went by fairly quickly; Isaac ate tacos with his family, and afterwards they all watched T.V together. They started to count down the days until their favorite show, Doctor Who, had its season premier. They all loved to watch the show, and its drama actually brought them closer together as a family.

That night, Isaac gazed at his ceiling, thinking about everything that had happened in his life. He had originally had the dream of Lucy dying, and it escalated rapidly from there. It went from random dreams happening to them all adding up, all to the conclusion of him learning that the people he trusted were fake. Luckily, they had discovered what they had done wrong, and they made up for it by fighting for their lives, all to stop Matt from taking over the world. It had been unbelievably close, and just as it seemed like there was no hope, things looked up, and it was murdered.

He wanted to think more about this, but the exhaustion from the previous days caught up to him, and he fell asleep, knowing that he would finally be able to dream in peace.

The days that followed went by fairly quickly. Isaac went to school like he always did, but the thought of Andre's surgery always sat in the back of his mind. The surgery hadn't been attempted many times before, and it had never been done successfully. It required Andre's skin to be almost completely transplanted, something that seemed almost impossible. It would be a revolution in science if it was actually a successful operation.

Finally, it was the big day, and Isaac sprang out of his bed. He ate crepes with his family like he always did, but no one did anything but watch T.V until it was time to say goodbye to Andre before the risky surgery. At 2:00 in the afternoon, everybody climbed into the family vehicle, and they were off, traveling to the hospital.

The family arrived in the hospital, and they checked in. They had been scheduled to meet with Andre at precisely 2:15, the time that they had arrived. Isaac and his family were led to the room where Andre was, and he got to walk in alone first. He saw him lying on the bed, in stable condition, but his skin was entirely red and black, just like it had been earlier. He walked over, a tear sliding down his cheek. He didn't have much to say, but he needed to say something.

"Andre... You've been my friend throughout almost this whole experience. You need to remain strong; I know you can do this. Please, remain strong, please! But, unless if you have anything to say, then... I guess this is goodbye."

"Isaac, I'm so sorry for earlier again. I promise, I will try to stay alive. As you know, I'm... I'm very stubborn... he he. Still... I don't know if I'll make it... My skin's b-burned pretty badly, and I have to be placed on a cold cloth in order not to scream in agony. I just need you to know, that this might be the last time I see you... so... I guess this really is goodbye."

"Goodbye, Andre." Isaac said, still slightly crying. He walked out of the room, and after a few minutes of his parents talking to him, one of the doctors walked over. They were moved into the waiting room, where they would have to sit and wait in the dark until Andre was done being operated on.

The next eight hours passed by as slowly as sap sliding down a tree, and Isaac tried not to think about Andre the whole time. Still, that was impossible, and he knew that he was just going to have to bear with a never ending fear.

After hours of sitting and waiting, the door opened slowly, and one single doctor walked in. His expression was solemn and sad, and Isaac shuffled over, knowing what the news would be. His parents walked over as well, and the doctor addressed all of them. "I'm sorry, Mr. and Mrs. Crowley, and Isaac... but... your concerns have come true. The surgery had been a failure. I'm sorry."

Isaac's heart dropped. Time seemed to stop moving, and he looked around, thinking that this was all just a dream. Still, he knew that it wasn't, and the drive home was completely silent. No one said a word as the car pulled into the driveway. Instead, he rushed to his room, slamming the door shut. He wasn't depressed, but he needed some time to himself. His best friend had died, and he knew that he had no one to really talk to besides his parents.

Isaac thought about his whole journey, his experience. He had started out as someone ignorant about the cosmos, but now he seemed to know so much more, having the information that almost nobody else had. He pulled Lucy's good luck charm out of his pocket and held it close to his heart once again, and he said a silent prayer to whatever was out there. He almost wanted to travel back in time, but he knew that there was no way he could. He had learned so much, and he could still learn more. He wanted to explore the universe, to learn the secrets of time. He knew that he could do it. He knew that there was an enormous amount of information, hidden away in the cosmos.

All he had to do was find it.

He pulled the blankets over his body, and he gazed up at the ceiling for the very last time in his adventure, his eyes stinging. He had come so far, and it was now finally over, all of it. He had won, but it was only at a price. His life had returned back to normal, and he was finally able to focus on other things, like his schoolwork. He thought about Andre, Lucy, and all of his other lost friends once again, but he was overwhelmed by these thoughts, and he fell asleep for the very last time, finally having closure to his adventure.

ARI LOHR

About the Author

Ari Lohr was born in Pensacola, Florida, but he moved to Portland, Oregon shortly after. He is currently 13 years old, and is an 8th grader. Some things he likes to do are read, write, and cook as many things as possible. While this is his first book, he plans to write many more.

ARI LOHR